THE STATEN ISLAND BUTCHER

George R. Hopkins

DEDICATION

To Marty and Helen
and
all the Silver Schlertoes

THE COMFORT I found in other friends – and the pleasure I had with them in things of earth – did much to repair and remake me. […] All kinds of things rejoiced my soul in their company – to talk and laugh and do each other kindnesses; read pleasant books together, pass from lightest jesting to talk of the deepest things and back again; differ without rancor, as a man might differ with himself, and when most rarely dissension arose find our normal agreement all the sweeter for it; teach each other or learn from each other; be impatient for the return of the absent, and welcome them with joy on their homecoming; these and such like things, proceeding from our hearts as we gave affection and received it back, and shown by face, by voice, by the eyes, and a thousand other pleasing ways, kindled a flame which fused our very souls and of many made us one.

~ St Augustine of Hippo, *The Confessions*, Book Four

CONTENTS

ACKNOWLEDGMENTS

My journey to the completion of this novel has been long and, at times, tortuous. I hope you find your journey through this story satisfying. I am most grateful to a number of very special people who helped me with their knowledge, expertise, and encouragement along the way.

In particular, I thank Dr. Louis Gianvito, Judge Charles A. Kuffner Jr., David Lehr, Mary von Doussa, Robert Boyd, Lenore Puleo, Jean Roland, and the Lacey's Book Club members for their technical assistance and their inspiration.

I also thank the many colleagues and friends who read the manuscript and offered concrete suggestions and encouragement. I would be remiss and in a lot of trouble, however, if I failed to thank my wife Diane and my children, Michael, Eileen, Mary, and Patrick, and my grandchildren who stuck by me as I wandered in and out of the story and the characters as I revised and edited it.

Thank you all.

I

Staten Island, New York

It was Indian summer in New York. After a series of sub-freezing days that included some snow flurries, Mother Nature challenged the *Farmers' Almanac's* predictions of a harsh winter with an unexpected softball of an amazing few days of warmth and sunshine.

Sophia Bellini savored the sunlight. She brushed her blond hair back and admired the clear blue skies. Coming home from work at Trader Joe's, she changed into her running clothes and set out for her long run of the week. The New York City Marathon was fast approaching. For the past few years, she had seen the runners assembling at Fort Wadsworth at the foot of the Verrazano-Narrows Bridge. She had mingled among the runners and caught their enthusiasm. Now at twenty-one years of age and in the best shape of her life, she wanted to be part of the experience.

Sophia's ex-boyfriend ran the marathon twice. He told her about the men urinating over the side of the bridge less than a mile from the start, about the sounds of "The Eye of the Tiger" playing along Fourth Avenue in Brooklyn, and about hitting "the wall" in Central Park. She remembered Dr. Gambella, her college professor, quoting Tennyson:

> "I am a part of all that I have met;
> Yet all experience is an arch wherethro'
> Gleams that untravell'd world whose margin fades
> Forever and forever when I move."

She didn't understand the quote then, but now she embraced it. She wanted to run the New York Marathon.

Sophia knew she needed to prepare for the 26.2 mile run through the five boroughs of New York City. There can be a loneliness in the long distance runner's training schedule, but she cherished it. Running was fun for Sophia. She enjoyed the solitude and the rhythm of a good run. Sometimes her runs were difficult. Her knees hurt. Her feet burned. Her shoulders tensed up. But when she got into what she called her "rhythm," it was peace and tranquility. When she hit that "rhythm," a feeling of happiness, almost ecstasy, flowed over her.

Right from the start of her run this late afternoon, she realized this was one of those special days. Her body fell into a controlled pace. Her breathing was even. Her legs moved freely. She seemed at times to be almost floating as she ran.

Soon, Sophia found herself running along Staten Island's South Beach boardwalk. In 2012, the deadly Hurricane Sandy wrought billions of dollars in damages and destroyed much of the boardwalk. As part of the rebuilding process, the boardwalk had been restored and a long dune was constructed along the 2.5 mile stretch hopefully to ward off future devastating hurricanes.

A warm ocean breeze embraced her as she ran. She smelled the salt sea. She smiled. It was like she was a kid again. As her feet beat a steady rhythm on the boardwalk, she smiled again. She was "feeling groovy." To her left were two small islands. She knew they were manmade islands which were long ago abandoned. Hoffman Island was the larger of the two measuring about eleven acres. It was covered with thick vegetation and had become almost a sanctuary for egrets, ibises, gulls, herons, cormorants, and occasionally even winter seals.

Swinburne Island is only about four acres in size and looks like a bombed out cluster of houses and debris. In the late 1800s and early 1900s, both islands served as quarantine stations for immigrants with symptoms of contagious diseases. Swinburne Island even had a hospital and crematorium. Today both islands are deserted and trespassing on the islands is prohibited.

Sophia, however, had been on both islands. Her then boyfriend rowed out to Hoffman Island last summer ostensibly for a picnic, but the birds attacked them. When they moved on to the more desolate Swinburne Island, her boyfriend attacked her and became her ex-boyfriend. Sophia fought him off and left him clutching his genitals on a pile of rocks as she swam the mile to shore.

She looked at the islands in the distance and decided to stop for a moment by the water. She left the boardwalk and walked under it to the shoreline. She loved the water and the sound of the waves gently rolling onto the beach. She smiled. She was what her mother would call "an Island person." In the distance she saw Coney Island and recalled the fun times her family had there.

Walking back under the boardwalk, she was thinking of the route she would take back home. She wasn't thinking of danger. She smiled at the sound of footsteps on the boardwalk above her.

Then she thought she heard footsteps in the sand behind her. She turned. No one was there. Her mind was playing tricks with her. She needed to get home. Her brother and his wife were coming over to the house tonight and her mother was cooking her special meatballs. She started to feel hungry. Her stomach growled.

Then she heard something behind her again.

She turned. He was right behind her. She frowned. He was too close to her. He smiled and they locked eyes. She brushed her hair back. Her forehead was damp from perspiration. Her hand started to shake. "Can I help you?" she said taking a step back.

He grinned. "You will, sweetheart. You definitely will." He and sprang forward like a cat on a mouse. A cold, hard hand gripped her around the throat and another placed a cloth with a pungent smell over her mouth and nose. Sophia Bellini felt her arms and legs relax and then blackness covered her like a dark, cold shadow.

*   *   *   *

A month later, Otto Grub walked into a Staten Island restaurant by the water called, appropriately enough, The Waterview. He asked for a table by the window for two. As the maître d' walked him to a table looking out on the Kill van Kull and a cluster of oil storage tanks across the choppy waters, a large Japanese container ship strove through the waters assisted by a Moran tug boat. He sat down and remembered when this now elegant restaurant had once been a neighborhood working class restaurant. The view of the water was always impressive. At night when the large ships glided by the windows, it conveyed a feeling of awe and peace.

But this was afternoon. The gray skies of November hung over the white storage tanks in the distance like an ominous harbinger.

"May I help you, sir?"

He looked up and observed a young blond waitress: approximate age – 24; height – 5' 6"; well-endowed; possibly 36" breasts; 26" waist; most likely a college student. Her name tag read, "Gretchen."

Grub noticed things. She wore large hoop earrings, probably brass, a plain brass ring on the thumb of her left hand and two on the pinkie of her right. When she handed him the menu, he observed a few small tattoos. The Viking symbol of two chevrons was on the inside of her right middle finger. On the wrist of her right hand was an open triangle. On the wrist of her left hand was a half-moon, half-sun tattoo.

Grub noticed things. It was both a gift and a curse. He saw a number of tattoos in his line of work. Some were beautiful. Some, he thought, were just plain stupid. He often wondered whether the human canvasses knew the meaning of the ink impregnated into their skin. The Viking symbol stood for creating one's own reality. The unclosed triangle meant open to change. The moon and sun symbol represented the merging of opposites, the dance of good and evil, a modern version of Yin Yang.

He stared at her face. A small dragonfly tattoo clung to her neck. She wore no makeup.

She placed a glass of water and a menu on the table and asked, "Would you like to order a drink, sir?"

He never understood tattoos. He had seen them all over people's bodies. They weren't new. They had been around for a long time. Winston Churchill had an anchor tattooed on his arm. Churchill's mother had a small snake around her wrist.

"Can I bring you something to drink, sir?" she repeated with a Disney-like smile.

"Yes. Two Pinot Grigios and a glass of ice. I am expecting another person for lunch."

"Do you have a preference, sir?"

He stared into her bosom. "Santa Margarita, thank you." As she walked away, he watched her tight buttocks.

"You're still a dirty old man, Grub," a tall, slender blond said sliding into the seat across from him.

"You're late."

"You're horny."

"I ordered a Pinot Grigio for you."

"Thank you. Did you get the equipment I told you to get?"

"You look beautiful, Suadela."

"You're horny. Answer my question. Did you get it or not?"

He rubbed his hands together. "It came today."

The waitress returned with the drinks. "Do you want to order now?"

"No. We'll wait awhile. Thank you."

Gretchen rolled her eyes and sighed. His eyes followed Gretchen as she left.

"Pay attention, shit-head. If you're going to continue this, you need to be more careful."

Grub clicked his glass against hers. "Up yours, Suadela." He raised his glass and took a long sip.

"They're looking for you, Grub. If you're not more careful, they'll catch your sorry ass."

"They haven't got me yet. And they never will." He turned his head and looked for Gretchen. "I'm enjoying this. It's become almost an obsession."

Suadela looked down at her drink and whispered, "I

have to go."

He leaned forward. "What are you talking about? You just got here. You haven't touched your drink."

"See those people who just came in. I know one of them. I think he'll recognize me."

Grub looked over her shoulder. There were three men being escorted to another table by the window. "They look familiar. Who are they?"

"It's the taller one. He was a priest at Our Lady of Good Counsel. I must go."

"But you just got here. We have things to talk about."

She rose slowly. Her look sent shivers down his spine. "I'll see you tonight."

He avoided her eyes and gazed out the window. A white twin screw tug, named the Harry McNeal, powered towards the Goethals Bridge. "Have you picked your next one?" Suadela whispered.

He motioned his head toward the table behind her. The waitress was bringing the men water and menus. "Gretchen will do fine."

$$* \quad * \quad * \quad *$$

The tall man in the black suit and Roman collar asked, "Well, what do you think about it?"

One of the men looked around the restaurant. He wore a worn olive green U. S. Army field jacket. The tattered patches on his arm displayed his former unit and rank. He ran his fingers through long, matted gray hair. His lips and mouth were black. "It's nothing like the old place I remember."

"I thought you'd get a kick out of it, Sergeant. The new owners have done so much since they bought it."

The third man folded his arms around his brown leather

jacket. "I don't like it."

"What's not to like?" the sergeant said. His voice was hoarse. He rubbed his straggly beard. "The place is clean, warm, and the view is great. I hope the fucking food's good."

"Don't mind my brother, Sergeant. He would find fault with anything I suggest. Thomas and I never seem to agree on very much."

The waitress arrived with water and menus. "May I bring you gentlemen a drink while you decide?

Thomas spoke first. "Do you have any Becks?"

"Of course, sir. And you, gentlemen?"

The old soldier hesitated, and Jack said, "We'll both stay with water, thank you."

"Of course," the waitress said as she turned.

"Come on, Jack, what's with this fucking water routine? You weren't like this when I met you at Benning. Today calls for a fucking celebration. We haven't seen each other in years."

"A lot has changed in those years, Malchus. How long have you been living on the streets?"

"Don't mind my brother, Sarge. He's got a messiah complex. Being a priest changed him." Thomas Cavanaugh tapped his fingers on the table and stared at the ceiling. "This place is so different. I really liked the old place. Why did they have to get rid of the tin ceiling tiles and old-fashioned ceiling fans connected by those cloth fan belts? It added character to the place."

"I think they call it progress, Thomas."

The waitress returned with the Becks beer and some bread. She stared at the priest for a moment too long.

"Is there something wrong?" Jack asked.

"Of course, no, I mean. It's none of my business, but you look very much like a teacher I had in high school. His name was Mr. Bennis."

"Did he hit on you, sweetheart?" Anthony smiled reaching for the bread and knocking over the candle holder as he stared at her breasts.

"You're Gretchen Leone, aren't you? You were in my English class at Garfield Academy. How are you doing?"

Gretchen's eyes widened and her mouth dropped. "The rumors were you were a priest, but I never believed them. How? I mean, why…?"

"It's a long story, Gretchen. That was a difficult time for everyone there." He motioned to Thomas. "This is my brother, Tom Cavanaugh. You may have seen him on the campus back then. He was a homicide detective. And this other man is a friend I met a long time ago in the service, Sergeant Malchus Anthony."

"But you're a priest?"

"Guilty as charged. But how are you doing?"

"I'm going to college, Mr. Bennis. I mean, Father. I'm planning on majoring in theatre and speech. I work here to help pay the tuition."

"Call him whatever the hell you like, sweetheart, except late for breakfast," the soldier mumbled. He pulled a black laced silk cloth from his pocket and blew his nose. His eyes stayed riveted on Gretchen Leone's breasts.

"What happened back at Garfield affected a lot of people. It was a horrible trauma. You were in Mark Anderson's class, weren't you? I'm so sorry about what happened to him."

"He was a good friend of mine. I didn't really know Susan Lewis."

Cavanaugh shook his head. It was a memory he wished he could forget. He scanned the restaurant. He noticed a middle age man in a gray striped three-piece suit staring at them. Or was he staring at Gretchen? Or maybe his brother? He saw two glasses of white wine on his table. There was something about the man that bothered Cavanaugh. It was a sixth sense he had developed from years as a New York City cop. It was like a persistent cold; he couldn't get rid of it. The man was immaculately dressed, but something was off. His brother would say Cavanaugh was crazy, and maybe he was – a little bit. As his brother and the waitress talked and Anthony leered at Gretchen and filled his mouth with rolls, Cavanaugh studied the stranger. Maybe it was his slick black hair and thin, curved moustache that made him look like a silent movie villain. The man's skin was pale and his mouth seemed to curve into a curious smirk.

Outside, the dark November clouds moved closer. Another cargo ship labored against the Kill van Kull current and threw a shadow across the windows. The ship's name was Stephano and it brought back instant thoughts about his son, Stephen. Thoughts about the mysterious stranger in the gray three-pieced suit, or the homeless veteran his brother brought with him, or his brother's purpose in bringing him out to lunch vanished. His son was sick. Stephen had a fever that wouldn't go away. The doctors in the Urgent Care thought it was viral, but it had persisted for almost two weeks. And now Stephen had developed conjunctivitis, his tongue looked swollen, and he was constantly crying. His wife Fran planned to take him to see her family doctor, Dr. Gianvito, today.

Cavanaugh grabbed his bottle of beer and swallowed hard. He should be with his wife and child, not here listening to a homeless alcoholic and his brother reminisce about old times.

"Check out the menu, Sergeant," the priest said. "This treat is on us. Personally, I like the lamb burger. It comes with caramelized Vidalia onions and zucchini sticks, but you make your own choice."

The old soldier's hands were shaking. "I don't understand why the fuck you're doing this. We were never really tight.

Why are you being so fucking kind?"

"I recall the night a long time ago when we met at Ft. Benning. There was a lot of drinking going on that night and a lot of stories. I wear a different uniform now, but I recognized your unit patch. You don't see many of those around these days. You were in the 11th Infantry Brigade in Vietnam, weren't you?"

Anthony stared out the window and drifted somewhere. He clasped his hands. "1st Platoon, Charlie Company, 1st battalion, 20th Infantry Regiment, 11th Infantry Brigade...."

"It must have been horrific."

"It was and still is. I live it every day. It's like I stepped in dog shit and I can't get rid of it."

Cavanaugh stood up abruptly. "I'm not much into this army chitchat. If you'll excuse me, my son is sick, and I really need to be with him and my wife. I'll leave you two to discuss military matters and how to save the world." He reached over and shook Anthony's hand. It was hard and weathered. "It's been *interesting* meeting you, but I have to go. Eat well and don't sweat; my brother will pick up the tab."

As they watched him leave, Father Bennis said, "He doesn't understand, Sergeant."

"Most people don't. In fact, I'm not sure I understand either. Sometimes I wonder if I'll ever understand what the fuck happened at Mai Lai."

* * * *

Cavanaugh drove straight home. It was dark when he arrived and the house was completely dark. He parked in the driveway and sat for a moment looking at the leaves blowing through the dilapidated cemetery next door. Maybe it was a mistake to buy a house next to a cemetery.

Where were his wife and son? He should have stayed

home. Where were they? Why didn't Fran call him? He had a bad feeling. Lately, he had been having a lot of bad feelings.

As he started to get out of his car, his cell phone rang. He fumbled in his pocket for the phone. It was Fran.

"Where are you?" he blurted out. "I just got home. What's happening? Where are you?"

Fran spoke softly and swiftly. There were beeping sounds in the background and loud voices.

"Where are you, Fran? I can't hear you."

"I'm in the hospital, Tom. They rushed Stephen here."

"Why? What happened?"

"Dr. G. thinks Stephen may have some rare Japanese disease I can't pronounce."

"Where are you, Fran? What the hell are you talking about? What's all that noise going on? Where are you?"

"I'm in the Emergency Room." Her voice broke up. "He could die, Tom! I took him to Dr. G. He diagnosed it, but the doctors here don't know their asses from their elbows. They don't know what they're talking about. They've never seen a case like his. Apparently, it's rare."

Cavanaugh stared at the shifting shadows in the cemetery.

"Are you still there, Tom?"

"Yeah, Fran. I'm coming. Where's Dr. G? Can you get ahold of him?"

"I called him. He's on his way."

Cavanaugh put the car in reverse. "I'm on my way, Fran. Hang in there. Tell Stephen I love him."

*   *   *   *

Gretchen Leone left The Waterview Restaurant at closing. It had been a long day. Kathy Flynn called in sick, and Gretchen worked a double shift. A cold, steady rain chilled her as she left the restaurant. Now she regretted walking from Randall Manor to work. It was only a couple of miles away. At the time, it seemed like a good idea. She wanted to shed a few pounds and walking was good exercise. But work and weather turned against her.

She was tired, but the tips had been good, and she wanted to share the news that she had met her old English teacher, Mr. Bennis, and that the rumors were true. He really was a priest. She had texted her boyfriend and her best friends about Mr. Bennis, and now she wanted to share the news with her grandmother.

She stepped in a deep puddle crossing Snug Harbor Road and cursed looking down at her new brown suede shoes. They were ruined. She recalled her grandmother's familiar saying, "Look on the bright side, dear. Never ask if your cup is half full or half empty. Be grateful you have a cup. No matter how bad things seem, there is a blessing in there somewhere. The goal is to find it." Gretchen looked down at her soaked feet. "Maybe now I'll have a good excuse to get that pair of black leather boots I wanted."

Her grandmother was the eternal optimist. When her mother and father divorced, her grandmother encouraged both her mother and her to think positively. "You are both better off without him," she insisted. "Every cloud has a silver lining. You just have to go through the clouds to find it."

When her mother died in a car crash on the Staten Island Expressway from a drunk, unlicensed driver, Gretchen's grandmother said, "It's God's will. Your mother is in a better place now. She is at peace. God called her home, and we'll see her again in the next world."

Gretchen did not know where her grandmother found her

strength, courage, and faith. She was always there for her. One thing she did know was her grandmother was a survivor. When Nanna's own mother died of uterine cancer in Americus, Georgia, she left her alcoholic, abusive father and worked her way to New York to build a new life. Gretchen imagined how difficult it must have been for her. Where her grandmother found her faith and determination, she did not know. She smiled again thinking about telling her about Fr. Bennis. She thought her grandmother would like the priest.

Gretchen wrapped her arms around her chest and shivered in the rain. She put her head down and quickened her pace. Amid a downpour of rain, she had the nagging feeling she was forgetting something. It was like an itch that came and went. She still had that term paper to write for her sociology class.

Thoughts raced through her head like a flock of frightened sparrows. At first, it started as a vague feeling, and she dismissed it. As the wind increased, however, the feeling increased. She felt someone was following her. She stopped at the corner of Kissel Avenue and Walnut Street and turned. The street was empty.

She walked faster. It was late, and the night was cold, wet and dark. There was no one else on the street. She recalled recent headlines in the *Staten Island Advance* about a missing girl named Sophia and about the police finding parts of a girl's body floating in Martling's Pond which was a little over a mile away.

Who would do something like that? Her grandmother often said there were a lot of sick people in the world today. Gretchen wondered why. Were the numbers of "crazies" in the world increasing or were they always there, hiding just beneath the headlines?

She wiped the rain from her eyes. The feeling of being

followed persisted. She could hear her grandmother's voice warning her about watching horror movies at night, "An overactive imagination, dear, can get you in trouble."

She smiled again. Mr. Bennis once wrote on one of her compositions, "Use your imagination more." He should meet her grandmother, she thought.

Then she heard it. It was a car slowing up alongside of her. She walked faster. The car followed her. She was about to start running when the car's window opened, and a voice called out, "Gretchen, how would you like a ride?"

She paused.

"It's a miserable night. I can give you a lift. I'm going your way."

She recognized the voice, but she couldn't see into the car.

"Come on, sweetheart. You're getting soaked. Let me give you a ride home. You'll catch your death of cold."

It was a phrase her grandmother would have used. The voice was familiar, but she could not place it. He knew her name. Why not?

As she ducked her head getting into the car, she recalled her grandmother's stern advice, "Never get into the car of a stranger." But as the door locks checked down, and she recognized the stranger, it was too late.

* * * *

Dr. Gianvito approached the child in the bed while a group of young interns observed him examining the boy. Fran and Cavanaugh looked on from the doorway with two nurses. "The onset of this illness starts with fever and looks very much like it's viral or the flu, but the persistent fever, red eyes, and swollen lymph glands remind me of several cases of Kawasaki I've seen in the past. The peeling of skin on the hands and feet and the rashes on his body add to this diagnosis."

"I never heard of this Kawasaki disease," a tall, thin, redheaded doctor with wire glasses admitted.

Dr. G. patted young Stephen's head. "It's rare. It's also known as mucocutaneous lymph node syndrome. We don't know what causes it, but the blood vessels in the child's body become inflamed. The symptoms are all there. I would suggest an ultrasound of the heart and blood tests just to make sure."

"Will he be all right, Dr. G.?" Fran cried from the doorway.

Everyone turned to Dr. G. He scratched his head. "Barring any complications, he should do well."

"What complications?"

Silence fell on the room.

Dr. G. cleared his throat. "Occasionally, the disease attacks the coronary arteries and could cause arterial aneurysms. But this is rare."

"What is the appropriate treatment?" a short, chubby female intern with a laptop asked.

"With high doses of aspirin and immunoglobulin, the fever usually goes down, and the prognosis of a full recovery is good." He lowered his voice and looked at Fran. "He should be fine, Fran. Don't worry."

Cavanaugh reached for Fran's arm, but she pulled away and ran down the hall.

* * * *

Father Bennis drove to Cavanaugh's house to talk with him. The house was shrouded in darkness. He let himself in by the back door and put on a pot of coffee. Where was everyone? He looked for a note, but there was none. He went into the living room and opened up the Bible. He started reading Luke's gospel when he came upon the passage where Jesus tells his disciples not to worry. But Bennis was worried. Where had his brother, Fran, and baby gone? Had something happened to little Stephen?

He was about to dial his brother's cell phone when he heard a car in the driveway and saw the headlights flash across the kitchen window. He was surprised when Cavanaugh came in alone.

"Where have you been? What's going on?"

"Stephen's in the hospital."

"What happened?"

"He's got some rare disease called Kamikaze or something like that."

"I doubt it's Kamikaze. They were Japanese suicide bombers in World War II."

"Well, whatever it is, it's serious and can damage his coronary arteries."

"Where's Fran?"

"She's with Stephen."

"Why aren't you with them, too?"

"You've got a million questions tonight, don't you? The simple reason is she's pissed off at me! She thinks I abandoned them when I went to meet you. She smelled beer on my breath and thought I was out drinking all day. That was the only thing I had the entire day! When I asked her if she wanted to get something to eat, she called me insensitive and indifferent to our son's condition." He threw the car keys at the wall. "It's all your God damn fault!"

"My fault? I wanted to talk with you about Stephen. I could see Fran was very upset and stressed out. I thought I could help."

"Bull shit! Where does your drunken, homeless,

perverted soldier friend fit in?"

"Come off it, Thomas. I saw Sgt. Anthony begging for food outside a supermarket on Forest Avenue. I didn't want to offer him money so I offered to buy him a meal. We had planned to go to a late lunch at The Waterview anyhow. I thought you wouldn't mind."

"He's a creep!"

"You have no idea what he went through. When I spoke to him, I didn't recognize him, but he recognized me. We met in a bar in a small town outside of Ft. Benning when I was in the service. There was a lot of drinking going on that night, and I don't remember much. I woke up in a motel room with a big headache."

"Did you think you were going to rescue this bum?"

"Thomas, you're doing what Fran did to you. You're judging him without knowing the whole story. He went through a lot in Vietnam."

"So did a lot of other people."

"His unit was involved in the Mai Lai Massacre. He saw innocent men, women, and children mowed down with machine guns and grenades. Some of the villages were shot in the head as they were crying and kneeling in prayer. He saw people pushed into a ditch and then shot. He witnessed women cradling babies slaughtered with indiscrimination. Some women threw themselves on their children to protect them and when they were shot, their bodies were moved and the children murdered. The soldiers destroyed the villagers' wells, killed their livestock and burned their hootches. He witnessed a lot of bad things at Mai Lai. He still can't get the images of the carnage out of his mind.""Bad things happen in war."

"Bad things happen in peace time, too." Bennis picked up the Bible he was reading. "There's a passage in Luke's gospel about the crowd that came to arrest Jesus at the

Garden of Gethsemane. Peter is said to have taken his sword and cut off an ear of one of the High Priest's slaves. Do you know the name of that servant?"

"What is this? *Jeopardy*? Let me take a wild guess. Van Gough?"

"His name was Malchus."

"So what?"

"Sergeant Anthony's first name is Malchus."

Cavanaugh stared at his brother and shrugged his shoulders. "And what the hell is that supposed to mean?"

"The point is war is full of cruelty and horror. A lot of people get hurt and carry physical and emotional wounds with them throughout their lives. Robert E. Lee once said, 'It is well that war is so terrible, otherwise we should grow too fond of it.'"

"Well, if Lee were still around, you could tell him it hasn't stopped people from having wars, and it probably never will."

"What I'm trying to say is that Sergeant Anthony is as much a victim as the High Priest's slave and the innocent villagers in Vietnam and in all the other wars around the world."

Cavanaugh went to the liquor cabinet and poured himself a large scotch. "Yeah, I hear you, except the villagers in Mai Lai are dead, and your bosom buddy Anthony is still alive. He had a part in those killings. He has his nightmares for good reason!"

"Thomas, you don't know what's going on in someone else's head. You weren't there. Unless you walk in the shoes of another, you don't know what they are going through. Ours is not to judge. Sergeant Anthony carries his guilt with him. I can't judge him. We all react differently to situations. I don't know what I would have done in his situation. He was carrying out orders."

"Come off it, Jack. That argument doesn't fly. It didn't at

Andersonville or at Nuremberg. Anthony's a murderer. Plain and simple. And a sick, perverted murderer to boot!"

Bennis closed his eyes and rubbed his forehead. "Look at it this way. Fran's feeling guilty about Stephen's sickness. Her reaction to you might be a result of the stress she is going through. People react differently to stress."

"In case you didn't realize it, brother, I'm going through stress, too. And that so-called friend of yours is a God-damn murderer and a sick, perverted murderer, too, if you ask me. I wouldn't be surprised if he were responsible for that missing girl's body they found in Martling's Pond the other day."

The priest shook his head. "You are being ridiculous, Thomas."

"Oh, you think so? I suppose you're going to tell me you didn't see the way he kept staring at the waitress's tits or that the black, silk laced handkerchief he blew his nose in was actually a pair of woman's panties!"

*   *   *   *

Father Bennis called the rectory at St. Peter's Church on St. Mark's Place to tell them he was staying the night at his brother's house. He went to the guest room, but could not get to sleep. He turned on the TV and watched the late night news. Eleanor Rosenbaum, a young reporter from Eyewitness News, stood in front of the 120 Precinct and reported that, according to unnamed sources, the body parts of the woman found in Martling's Pond were definitely not those of the missing Sophia Bellini.

An earlier interview with some members of the Curtis High School cross-country track team showed one of the students recounting details about finding one of the body parts. "At first, I thought it was a dead fish," a thin, acne-faced teenager said, "but then I saw it was an arm. It really shocked the hell out of me! I almost puked."

A film clip of Sophia Bellini's parents embracing each other and crying on the front steps of their house in Rosebank played as the reporter's voice-over commented, "Mr. and Mrs. Bellini are clinging to hope that their missing daughter will soon be found."

Leaning on an iron picket fence, a heavyset neighbor spoke about what at great kid Sophia was. "We all can't imagine what happened to her. Things like this don't happen in this neighborhood." He scratched a worn Seattle Sonic sweatshirt and shook his head. "She used to deliver our paper and walk our dog. We are all praying for her safe return. The Bellinies are good people. They don't deserve this."

Bennis turned the TV off. He stood looking at the blank screen. Does anyone deserve something like this? No one seemed interested in the unknown severed woman's body found floating in the pond. They didn't know her.

He had noticed Sergeant Anthony staring at Gretchen. He saw the black silk handkerchief but didn't realize it was a woman's panties. What was Anthony doing with women's underwear? Maybe it was nothing.

Did he really know the man? No. They met decades before. A lot happens. Things change. People change. Alternatives exclude. The Mai Lai Massacre left Anthony permanently scarred. But could he be involved with the dead girl? At Mai Lai some of the women villagers were raped before they were shot.

In the restaurant, Sgt. Anthony avoided all questions about his past. He devoured everything in sight. After eating a dozen raw oysters and a shell steak with mac and cheese, he ordered an Oreo crusted cheesecake. His persistent whining for a brandy on the rocks, however, went unheeded.

When he left to go to the Men's room, Bennis noticed the sergeant picked up the rolls and butter from the table and shoved them in his pocket.

The Old Testament lauded soldiers like Joshua, David, and Gideon. In the New Testament, there are four Roman soldiers mentioned and they are all men of integrity, decency, and honor. But his brother was right. He saw it time and again. We are God's children, but we are all different. Race, ethnicity, national origins, economic backgrounds do not exempt us nor excuse us from wrong doings. Soldiers are capable of moral corruptibility, as well as people from all other walks of life, including politicians, bankers, lawyers, teachers, and even police and religious.

Bennis stood staring at the TV as if in a trance. Can we ever really know another person? Do we all wear masks afraid to show others who we really are? Do we ever really know who we really are?

Did Sophia Bellini's parents and neighbor know who she was? Did they know the thoughts, desires, experiences, and secrets she buried from others?

He thought of his brother. On the outside, Thomas Cavanaugh looked like a hard-nosed, cynical ex-cop. But Bennis saw the hurt and frustration in his brother's eyes. Frustration leads to aggression. Aggression can sometimes be hidden inside or displayed outwardly. Bennis sighed. He sat on the bed and pulled out the pink Connemara marble Irish rosary beads his mother gave him when he entered the service. As he started to pray, he thought about how much his brother loved his wife and son. How could he get Thomas and Sergeant Anthony not so much to be consoled as to console and not so much to be understood as to understand?

* * * *

The Staten Island Butcher

The three-story timber framed Tudor style building seemed to blend into the darkness. Rain beat down on walls that held many secrets. In 1861, Captain John C. Quelch, a privateer who made his fortune smuggling arms and contraband to the Confederacy during the Civil War, designed and constructed the building. After Captain Quelch's death in a shipwreck off the coast of North Carolina, the house passed through many different hands. In the late 1800s, it was a guest house; in the early 1900s, a busy brothel; in the 1920s, a speakeasy; in the 1930s, a restaurant; in the 1940s a church.

Gunther Grub came to America during the 1956 Polish protests. He purchased the building and married Anastasia Savanaudis, a voluptuous, strongminded flirt who seduced him in a sleazy bar in Perth Amboy, New Jersey. Initially, the sex was good, but when Anastasia became pregnant, things changed. She demanded expensive clothes and extravagant goods. Her appetite for material things seemed insatiable. To make ends meet, Gunther often worked double shifts and nights at the U.S. Gypsum Plant on Richmond Terrace.

Otto was Gunther and Anastasia's only child. Otto was a "dream come true" for Gunther. He cherished his relationship with his son. Anastasia, on the other hand, displayed no love for the boy. He was a nuisance, a burden, an unfortunate mistake. Nothing Otto did was good enough for her. He cried too much. He ate too fast. He wet the bed. He left his clothes all over the place. Otto loved his father, but came to hate his mother.

Gunther believed in education and encouraged both Otto and his wife to take advantage of the education America offered. He was pleased when Anastasia enrolled in night classes at the local high school. Young Otto wondered why his mother never studied or had homework as he did. When his mother went off to "classes," Gunther would cook dinner for Otto and put him to bed. To make ends meet and to pay their increasing bills, Gunther would work overtime whenever he could. On those days, Anastasia would stay with Otto or, if she had school, hire a babysitter.

At work Gunther heard stories from some of the men about a woman named Anna who hung out in a local bar on Jersey Street.

"You should see this broad. She's a knockout and she will do anything for a few bucks – absolutely anything!"

"You gotta come with us some night, Gunther, and see this chick. She's unbelievable."

Curiosity got to Gunther, and one night, after a late shift, he went with some of the men to see the notorious "Anna" for himself.

Lars Jacobson pointed her out to Gunther. She was sitting at the bar with one arm wrapped around a man in an expensive herringbone suit. Gunther watched her nibbling at the man's ear and saw her other hand sliding up his leg. He saw her unzipper the man's pants and reach in.

Gunther smiled. The stories were true. But then he saw the woman's face reflected in the mirror behind the bar. It was his own Anastasia.

That night Otto woke up to loud shouts from the kitchen. He heard his father hollering, "How could you do this to me and Otto. I have given you everything, and this is what you do? And you leave Otto alone while you go out whoring! You're nothing but a God damn tramp and a slut!"

Anastasia's words cut through the walls and hit Otto like a dagger. "I never wanted that bastard! He is a waste of life, and you are a poor excuse for a man!"

There were more shouts and noise as pots and dishes were thrown about. Otto buried his head under his pillow. The muffled sounds continued for a few minutes, and then suddenly a deadly silence descended on the house.

Otto sat up in his bed and listened. The noises and the voices stopped. He turned over and went back to sleep.

In the morning, Gunther Grub cooked pancakes and bacon for Otto, packed his lunch, and sent him off to school. Otto never saw his mother again, and he never asked where she had gone. He never liked her. Things were more peaceful with her not around. He studied hard and took an interest in science. After high school, he went on to college where he pursued his fascination with the sciences. He wasn't sure where his fascination with science came from, but thought it may have started with his discovering a skull buried in their cellar.

After his father died, Otto earned his degree in mortuary science, and Captain John C. Quelch's old Tudor house soon underwent another change. It became the Grub Funeral Home.

*   *   *   *

"I gotta take a piss," Sgt. Anthony announced to Fr. Bennis in the restaurant. That was the last Bennis saw of him. Anthony slipped out of the restaurant, but not before he swiped the tip left by an elderly couple at the table behind him.

The rain poured down on him, but the urgency for a drink became overpowering. He didn't believe he had a drinking problem. He liked alcohol, and it dulled the images and sounds that haunted him. Meeting Jack Bennis, however, triggered a flood of memories and nightmares. He heard the cries of women and children murdered in Mai Lai. He saw the flames of village's huts soaring into the sky.

He pounded his head trying to obliterate the scenes flashing across his mind. He half-jogged to the closest liquor store. He knew where most of them were. Trying to stifle the noises in his brain, he sang a jingle from the past as loud as he could, "What's the word? Thunderbird. How's it sold? Good and cold. What's the jive? Thirty twice."

He arrived at the liquor store drenched to his skin. Instead of choosing Thunderbird, however, he picked up a bottle of the sweeter Richard's Wild Irish Rose from the bottom shelf. "This will be my special dessert," he said as he carried his bottle wrapped in a brown paper bag out of the store.

The rain beat down on him mercilessly. He needed shelter. Fortified with his Wild Irish Rose, he walked deliberately back toward Sailors' Snug Harbor where he pried open a loose gate and slipped into the Chinese Scholar's Gardens.

The Vietnam horrors slowly faded from his mind's eye as he savored the cherry sweet wine. Memories of a young Jack Bennis appeared. They started drinking beer that night in a small town not far from Ft. Benning. He remembered their building a pyramid of beer cans. Then Bennis pulled one from the bottom and they all crashed to the floor. The bartender, a tough redneck, didn't appreciate the mess, but Bennis insisted on buying drinks for the bar. That was when they switched to Jack Daniels. Anthony recalled how drunk Bennis became. He doubted Bennis remembered the women they met or how they all stumbled off to motel rooms close by. Anthony used all the money in Bennis' wallet to pay for the drinks, the motel rooms, and the girls.

Squeezing between the iron gates, Anthony heard a car slowing up on Kissel Avenue. He stumbled and fell behind some tall bamboo trees. He cursed that he might have been seen. Then he cursed again when he realized he dropped the bottle of Wild Irish Rose. As he fumbled in the undergrowth for the bottle, he heard the car stop. He froze. Like a sniper, he peered into the street's darkness. His hands shook. His vision was blurry. He thought he heard voices. Then a car door opened. Someone was getting into the car. He couldn't see who it was. Then suddenly the car skidded slightly as the driver sped away.

Sgt. Malchus Anthony exhaled. He picked himself up, found his bottle, and made his way to the peace and shelter of the scholar's study pavilion. He pulled out the black silk panties, held them to his nose, and inhaled deeply. He smiled. His conscious memories of the past diminished as he scrunched into a corner, drained the Wild Irish Rose and slipped into another night of semi-restless sleep.

* * * *

II

Jack Bennis woke up early the next morning. He was on a tight schedule. No time to shower. He wanted to talk with his brother and he needed to get to church to say the 9:00 a.m. Mass.

A quick check of the driveway showed Cavanaugh's car was gone. He reasoned he must have gone to the hospital to be with Fran and Stephen. Bennis started his car and headed down Arthur Kill Road toward St. Peter's.

His brother and Sgt. Anthony played on his mind. What do we really know about each other? He remembered Edwin Arlington Robinson's poem "Richard Cory." How many times had he taught the poem to oblivious high school teenagers? Everyone admired Richard Cory. He was a gentleman - rich, handsome, charismatic. They envied him. Then one calm summer night, Richard Cory went home and put a bullet through his head.

Who really knows what is going on in another's head? What drives them? Who can ever really understand what went on in the minds of the school shooters at Columbine High School, Stoneman Douglas High School and Sandy

Hook Elementary School?

Sgt. Anthony needed help. But how could he help him? He tried to remember the night he first met him. Images flashed through his mind like lightning bugs on a summer night. It had been hot that night. Bennis had just been paid. Some of the men in his unit drove to a bar somewhere off base. They had just returned from a difficult mission. It was a time to unwind. The mission was top-secret, and it had been messy. People were killed. He questioned his orders, but he carried them out.

There were deer heads mounted on the walls of the bar. His group met up with Anthony and some of his friends and they started drinking cans of Budweiser.

Somebody in the group that night started building a pyramid with the empty beer cans. The pyramid got higher and higher as the night went on. He remembered how good it was to relax, laugh, and enjoy the company of others. He could almost smell the stale beer odor of the bar.

There were bras, underwear, and hats hanging on the antlers on the walls. The bartender looked like a miniature Paul Bunyan with the attitude of a trapped, hungry mountain lion.

Someone pulled a beer can from the bottom of the pyramid. He recalled the laughter of the men he was with and the angry outburst of the bartender. To smooth things over, Bennis bought a round for everyone in the bar. But then the distant memories faded to darkness.

Jack Bennis' next memory of that night was waking up in a motel room the following morning. There was a sweet smell in the room. His clothes were neatly folded on the dresser, but his money was gone and so was Sgt. Anthony.

Pulling into the parking lot of St. Peter's, Bennis wondered what else happened that night. But that was in the past. He was a priest now, and Malchus Anthony was a man who needed help. What drove him to the streets? That Anthony had a problem was obvious to anyone who saw him, but not to him. Bennis knew Anthony would never get better until he recognized he had a problem. Why didn't he make use of help from the Veterans' Administration? Among the benefits the VA provides are treatments for medical conditions, mental illness, addiction abuse, post- traumatic stress disorder, and homelessness.

But Bennis knew Anthony must first realize his problems and then seek help. Acknowledging his own problem and his powerlessness to overcome it, led Jack Bennis to seek God's power. The guilt he felt for his own actions led him to seek reparation and reconciliation with God.

Bennis knew the statistics. Over half the homeless veterans have disabilities. Half suffer from mental illness. Two-thirds suffer from substance abuse problems.

Finding Anthony sleeping in the doorway of a supermarket with a used coffee cup and a torn cardboard "Help a Veteran" sign and his persistent pleading for a drink in the restaurant were clear signs of Anthony's problems. His clothes were filthy, his face unshaven, his hair long, dirty, and disheveled, his lips blackened, his hands shaking. But the way his brother saw Sgt. Anthony staring at the waitress and that black silk "handkerchief" he wiped his nose with gave Bennis additional concerns. Could this old, homeless veteran be responsible for the body parts found in Martling's Pond?

* * * *

Cavanaugh hated hospitals. He associated them with bad things. It wasn't the antiseptic smell or the hustling of nurses and aides in the halls, but the walls seemed to close in on him whenever he entered a hospital. People are sick and dying in a hospital. His brother once told him he suffered from nosocomephobia, the extreme fear of hospitals. Cavanaugh denied it, but avoided touching anything in the hospital. He believed that if he ever were admitted to the hospital, he would never come out alive.

His hands were sweating when he entered his son Stephen's room. On a chair by the bed, Fran slept. One hand was on Stephen's little arm. He looked around the room and saw a monitor and IV bags and a TV on the wall.

He pulled up a chair and asked Fran, "How are you doing?"

She opened her eyes with a start. "Better. He's finally sleeping. The doctor came in a little while ago. He said he's doing well and responding to the medicine."

"I'm sorry about last night, Fran. I was upset about what happened at the restaurant. I didn't mean to take it out on you."

Fran looked up at him. Her eyes were swollen. "You didn't take it out on me. I took it out on you. I'm sorry. This whole thing is too much. I don't know what to do."

"You're doing all you can. It's in the hands of the doctors and God now. I just want you to know I'm with you. We'll get through this together."

Fran started to sob and Cavanaugh reached over and hugged her just as the nurse walked into the room. "Hope I'm not disturbing something," she said moving to Stephen's bed. She was a tall brunette who spoke and worked with alacrity. "My name is Rosemary Palladino. I'll be the nurse assigned to Stephen today. If you need anything just call me."

As she checked the charts and the monitors, she looked up at the wall. "They tell me you've been here all night, Mrs. Cavanaugh. Why don't you go home and get some rest?"

"I can't. I have to be here."

"The little guy is in good hands. His fever is down and the IV seems to be working." She smiled and looked up at the television. "Why don't you turn the TV on? It will take your mind off things. We can't have the two of you making out in the hospital."

"I'm afraid it will wake him up."

"What? The making out or the television? The making out might do that, but you can mute the sounds on the television and watch the captions. You might as well use it. You're paying for it anyway." Nurse Palladino reached up and turned the TV on. "There, I put on the news channel. When Stephen wakes up you can switch it to cartoons."

As swiftly as she came in, the nurse left. Cavanaugh and Fran looked at each other and then at Stephen. He was sleeping. They both looked up at the TV. There was breaking news. Another group of unidentified severed body parts were found. This time they were in the Silver Lake Reservoir. Helicopter views of the reservoir showed police and ambulances at the scene. The captions indicated the police had no official comment, but sources suggested the victim was another young woman.

"Oh, my God!" Fran said. "I hope it's not that Sophia girl who's been missing."

Cavanaugh held his wife's hand. His back stiffened. He said nothing.

"What's happening, Tom? Why is this happening?"

His eyes moved from the TV, to Stephen, and then to Fran. "I've got a bad feeling, Fran. I think we're dealing with another serial killer."

* * * *

The night watchman at the Chinese Scholar's Garden was Chen Wong Yong, a nineteen year old student at the

The Staten Island Butcher

College of Staten Island. It was an easy job. The Chinese Garden was closed at night. His job was to patrol the grounds to prevent vandalism. He knew the reason he got the job was that his parents came from the city of Chongqing on the lower banks of the Yangtze River. Although his parents named him Wong Yong, which means brave, strong and indefatigable, he was known to all his friends as Jimmy Chen.

Jimmy loved his job because there wasn't much to do so he had time to study or sleep. All he really had to do was dress in his official "rent a cop" uniform and patrol the Chinese Garden. But since no one came to the garden at night, Jimmy settled himself into one of the pavilions with his laptop and his cell phone and would make a casual tour of the facilities a few times a night.

The heavy rains did not let up until around two o'clock in the morning. His laptop was running out of power. Looking outside he saw the rain had nearly stopped. He stood up and stretched. He was bored and stiff. He plugged his computer into an outlet and decided to take a walk around the grounds. It was a clear night, but it was cold and damp. He put on the official dark blue full length rain coat and a lightweight nylon bucket hat.

Jimmy looked at himself in the mirror and smiled. The coat was two sizes too large for his 135 pound body. If his girlfriend could see him, she would laugh hysterically. But no one would see him and his computer needed charging. The walk would wake him up.

He didn't care about the paintings and calligraphy in the garden or the plants or curved walkways or the fact that the wood used was joined together using traditional Chinese construction techniques without glues or nails. He never appreciated the peace and quiet of the gardens. The only thing that interested him was the Koi pond. He loved to watch the carp, or "gold fish" as he called them, swim to a point by one of the bridges and wait to be fed.

On his way to the pond, he walked through the Scholar's library. He saw something in the corner. It moved. He should have brought his flashlight.

Fear gripped him. He trembled. He stammered into the darkness, "Get out of here! You are not supposed to be here."

The object in the corner rose slowly. It made a grunting sound. It was a man in an old army uniform.

Jimmy's voice quivered, "Get out of here before I call the cops. You're trespassing."

Suddenly, the figure sprang at him. Jimmy backed away and tried to run, but the man's hands gripped his throat.

"You're dead!" the man exclaimed. "I killed you once. Get the fuck out of my life! Get out! Get out!"

The fingers squeezed harder and harder. Jimmy couldn't speak. He scratched at the man's unshaven face.

"You're dead," the man screamed. "I killed you. Go away. You're dead! You're all dead!"

Jimmy felt something snap in his neck and then it seemed like he was flying through darkness. Jimmy Chen was dead before he hit the water. As his body sank into the pond and the Koi swam to greet him, his ancestors might have seen the irony in Chen Wong Yong's Chinese name meaning "brave, strong, and indefatigable."

* * * *

Otto Grub woke up with a start. His phone was ringing. He rubbed his eyes and cursed. He checked the clock. It was 9:30 in the morning. Most people were up and out of the house by nine, but Otto had only gotten to bed at 6:30 a.m. It had been a long night and his body ached.

The phone kept ringing.

He swung his legs off the bed and stretched. Why was anyone calling him?

"Answer the phone, shit head," Suadela said.

"I'm tired. I worked hard last night. She was heavier than I expected. You think it's easy? It was a miserable night. I was soaked when I came in."

"All you ever do is bitch, bitch, bitch. I don't know why I put up with you!"

"Come on, Suadela, give me a break. I got her, didn't I?

"Where is she?"

"In our special room in the cellar. I stripped her and strapped her to the table. She gave me no trouble. The chloroform worked perfectly just like the others. She's better than I expected. She's a real beauty."

The phone kept ringing.

"Did anyone see you?"

"No. I was careful. I pay attention to details."

"The police found the others."

"So what? They can't identify them."

The phone continued ringing.

"Answer the God damn phone. It's driving me crazy."

Otto rose. His back ached. His nose was running. He wiped his nose with his left hand and reached for the phone with his right.

"Hello. Grub Funeral home. How can I help you?"

"Mr. Grub, I need your help. My son dead."

Otto grabbed a pen and started to take notes. "When did your son pass away, sir?"

"He not pass away. He murdered. Police call me this morning. His body found in Chinese Garden."

"Have the police released his body?"

"No. They doing some kind of tests. He in morgue."

"Have you identified the body? Are you sure it is your

son's?"

"No. Not yet. They find license on him. It's him. I know. He work at Chinese Garden."

"You are going to have to identify the body and there will be forensic tests. It may take a few days before your son's body is released."

"My wife go identify him. I want you arrange funeral."

Otto shook his head and frowned. He didn't need this. The voice sounded Asian. There would be special arrangements.

"Pardon my asking, sir, but why did you call me?"

"You funeral home. Right?"

"No. I mean yes, but why did you call the Grub Funeral Home. There are many other funeral homes on Staten Island."

"I call others. They not do Chinese funerals. They tell me call you."

Grub cursed under his breath. He looked at Suadela. She was beautiful. He shrugged and wiped his nose again. He took down the information. Chen Wong Yong, also known as Jimmy Chen, was nineteen years old. His body was in the Seaview Morgue. Grub knew the procedures to get the body and the special preparations needed for a Chinese funeral.

This was going to take time. The whole procedure and everything around it had to be done in a proper way. Irregularities in the funeral could cause bad luck to the deceased family. When he received the body, he would have to clean it and apply talcum powder on it. Since he did not die at home and was a young bachelor, he would be waked at Grub Funeral Home, not in his own home. Special yellow and white "holy" paper would be placed in the coffin to protect the body from dangerous spirits. Grub needed to provide a cloth for the mourners to be worn on their left sleeve.

He noticed things and paid attention to details. It would be a lot of work.

"Did you kill him?" Suadela asked. "The Chinese Garden is where you got your latest prize."

"No. Nobody saw me."

Grub looked at his notes. According to Chinese tradition, an older person must not show formal respect to a younger person. His parents may not come to the wake. He knew some Chinese families place a pearl in the mouth of the deceased to prevent his ghost from coming back.

Grub had a lot of work to do. Official invitations would need to be made indicating the funeral's date, time, and location. Mr. Chen wanted a small obituary composed indicating Jimmy's birth date, date of death, and family members. He also wanted to include a family tree.

He would need a picture of Jimmy to place on a table in front of the coffin with food offerings on the table and a central urn for joss sticks to be offered by guests as a sign of respect. And then there were the white envelopes for mourners to make cash donations to the family.

Arrangements for Jimmy Chen's funeral were going to take a lot of time. Damn those other funeral directors! At the last Chinese funeral he arranged, people stayed all night gambling. They claimed they were guarding the body and the gambling helped them stay awake during the vigil.

He wanted time to be with Gretchen, his latest prize. He sighed and shook his fists.

"Relax, Otto. Everything in its place. Gretchen will still be there and it will give you more time to dispose of Sophia Bellini. You can't keep cutting up the bodies and dumping them around the Island. Did you get that machine I told you about?"

"Damn it, Suadela, I told you I did!"

His head was pounding. He wanted to play with his latest prize. He needed time. Those other directors will pay for this. He smiled. "Maybe the next one will be one of their daughters!"

* * * *

Two unidentified female bodies and a missing teenage girl spurred on the belief there was a serial killer on Staten Island. The press, television, and radio fanned the fires and public outrage and hysteria caused the newly elected Mayor of New York, Don Juliano, to pressure Police Commissioner Arthur Forster to assign a special task force to find the killer or killers. The death of Jimmy Chen added to the panic.

When Gretchen Leone failed to come home, Greta Johnson, her grandmother, called the local precinct and spoke to the desk sergeant, P.O. Frances Cackowski. "My granddaughter hasn't returned from work," she explained. "This is not like her. I called her on her cell phone, but there was no answer. I am worried something might have happened to her."

Cackowski took down the information and promised they would look into it. She passed the details on to Detective Morton Goldberg, who had been assigned on temporary duty to investigate the unidentified body parts and the missing Sophia Bellini.

In view of the circumstances, Goldberg acted quickly. He called Mrs. Johnson, took some information from her about her granddaughter, and assured her he would look into the matter. He then drove to the restaurant where Gretchen worked. Larry Green, a short, overweight man with a pony tail and a slight twitch in his left eye, explained how one of the waitresses had called in sick and he asked Gretchen to work overtime. He said he spent most of the night assisting in the kitchen. "One of the waitresses found her cell phone. Apparently, she forgot it when she left. You might want to talk to her."

Goldberg thanked Green and interviewed the staff. He soon found everyone liked Gretchen. She was a good worker. She was everyone's friend. But no one actually saw her leave work.

Jose Rivera, one of the bus boys, was nervous talking to the police. When Goldberg assured him he was not with ICE (Immigration and Customs Enforcement) and was just trying to find out what happened to Gretchen, he recalled how hard it rained that night. "She only lives about a mile away. I think she walked to work. Maybe she walked home. I would have given her a ride if I knew she was going to walk home. She is a really nice person."

Maureen Ryan, a short brunette with sparkly blue eyes, told Goldberg, "I saw her phone in the ladies' room after she left. I was going to give it to her today."

"Do you know if she used her phone last night?"

Maureen checked over her shoulder to see where Mr. Green was. She looked down and whispered, "She texted her boyfriend and a lot of her friends. We all do when he's not looking, but last night she was in a good mood and was on the phone more than usual."

"Why? What was different about last night?"

"She saw her old English teacher."

"What was so special about that?"

"He's a priest. She had him as a teacher a couple of years ago and the rumor was he was a priest, but nobody believed it. When she saw him yesterday afternoon, she wanted to tell everyone she knew that the rumors were true!"

"Do you happen to know the school she went to?"

"I think it was Garfield. You know that place on the hill where the rich kids go."

Goldberg frowned. He knew it all too well.

"Oh, don't get me wrong. Gretchen wasn't rich. She won some kind of scholarship. She told me once that one of the boys in her class was killed there."

Goldberg and his former partner, Tom Cavanaugh, worked together on finding the killer who called himself *Lex Talionis.* He knew his brother Jack Bennis was a Jesuit priest who had been on leave from the priesthood when he taught at Garfield Academy at that time.

"Do you recall the name of this priest/teacher?"

"Are you kidding me? That's all she did that night. Whenever we had a break she talked about Mr. Bennis. I think she had a crush on him." Maureen reached in her pocket and handed Goldberg Gretchen's cell phone. "Here. You can check her texts to see what I mean."

Goldberg looked at Gretchen's phone. It had a decal of a unicorn on its case. He closed his eyes for a moment, and then asked, "Was this Fr. Bennis or Mr. Bennis with anyone?"

"Yeah, Gretchen said he was with his brother and some old guy in an Army uniform. I came in after they left so I didn't see them."

"Is there anything else you can tell me about them?"

"No, not really. Well, maybe one thing. Gretchen told me she saw the soldier guy swipe the tip from a table as he left."

"What did this soldier look like?"

"Sorry, Detective. I didn't see him. All I know is she told me he was old and dirty and smelled like rotten fish."

When Goldberg left the restaurant, he sat in his car and checked the text messages on Gretchen's phone. It wasn't much to go on, but it was a start and it was all he had so far. Scanning the text messages, Goldberg discovered a few things. Gretchen was excited about discovering the rumors that Jack Bennis was a priest were real. And Maureen was right that Gretchen did a lot of texting. The problem was some of it he could *almost* understand, but most of it he would need a translator for.

"GUESS WHO I MET 2N8 MR BENNIS HES REALLY A PRIEST!"

"he was with his bro and otl om"

"at wrrj saw bennis 2n8 hes a priest"

"UFB"

"B9 g2g ttul"

"uhgtbsm he a priest?"

"HFAC!"

"bm&y ficcl"

"sy2moro tbc"

"IDBI"

"ttyl"

"cus"

"ik uwr cut"

"ILU WYWH XOXOXO"

Goldberg scratched his head. He liked puzzles but this was like another language. Acronyms! Why don't young people write plain English? He closed the phone and looked out at the storage tanks across the Kill van Kull. He hadn't spoken much to Cavanaugh since he retired. They were always the odd couple when they worked together. Sometimes they were like oil and water.

Still, they were close and had shared a lot. He remembered Cavanaugh coming to their Hanukah celebrations and being best man at Cavanaugh and Fran's wedding.

He hated to involve him in this. Cavanaugh and his brother were like bulls in a China shop. Questioning them could be a real *tsuris*. He didn't like it, but it was part of the job and the only clue they had to the missing Gretchen and possibly to the serial killer the press had already dubbed "The Staten Island Butcher."

* * * *

When Fr. Jack Bennis arrived at fourteen month old Stephen Cavanaugh's hospital room, he carried a large Teddy bear. The child lay sleeping on Mickey Mouse and Minnie Mouse sheets surrounded by bright blue and pink walls decorated with various cartoon characters and smiley faces. A long colorful couch flanked by Big Bird and Cookie Monster nestled against the window. Red, yellow and blue balloons floated from the high side rails of his bed. Fran and Tom Cavanaugh sat holding hands on two leather armchairs beside Stephen's bed. The cheerful ambiance of the room contrasted with the intravenous tube in Stephen's hand, the oxygen tubes in his nose, and the monitors, blood pressure device, electric suction machine, oxygen tank, and defibrillator along the wall.

"How's he doing?" the priest whispered from the doorway.

"You didn't have to come, Jack?"

"He's my Godchild, Fran, and my nephew to boot."

Both Fran and Cavanaugh rose and motioned toward

the door. When they were in the corridor across from the nurses' station, Fran explained, "The doctors say he's improving. His fever is going down. Apparently the immunoglobulin they're giving him is working. Things are looking better. We were really scared. He looked so sick, so helpless."

"I thought maybe I could give him a blessing. I can't give him the sacrament of Anointing of the Sick because he's too young, but I can give him a blessing." He looked at his brother.

Cavanaugh shrugged. "I guess it can't hurt."

Fr. Bennis tiptoed over to Stephen's bed. He made the sign of the cross and began, "May almighty God, Father, Son, and Holy Spirit, bless this child. Please listen to our pleas and restore Stephen to health if such is Your holy will...."

Cavanaugh and his wife stood back at the door. Suddenly, Cavanaugh's cell phone rang. Fran shot him an angry look. He grabbed his phone, checked the number, and stepped into the corridor. Two nurses with charts in their hands were talking at the nurses' station. "I have to take this, Fran."

"If that's another one of those 'you qualify for a reduced rate on your credit cards' calls, and you wake up Stephen, I'm going to scream!"

"Easy, Fran. I think it's Goldberg. I'll take it outside."

"Why is *he* calling you now? You're retired."

"I won't know until I answer it." Cavanaugh walked down the hall and took the call by the elevators.

* * * *

"What's up, Morty? You got me at a bad time."

"I need to talk to you and your brother, Tom."

45

"Tom? Why so formal? You always call me Cavanaugh. You make this sound serious."

"I've been assigned to look into the murders and missing girls on the Island."

"Yeah, I saw that on the news. They found two cut up bodies and are looking for that Sophia girl. Did they find her?"

"No. But we now have another missing girl."

"Geeze Louise, it sounds like you've got a serial killer out there. But why call me? I retired."

"Well, that's just it. It seems you and your brother were two of the last people to see this missing person. She waited on you yesterday at The Waterview Restaurant."

"I don't know what we can tell you, Morty. I left early. I'm with Fran and my brother now in the hospital. Stephen's sick."

"I'm sorry to hear that…"

"So are we."

"But I need to talk to you and Jack."

"Maybe you didn't hear me, Morty. Our son is in the hospital. He's got some disease I can't even spell. It could be serious. I have nothing to tell you."

"Do you want me to send a patrol car to pick you up and take you to the station?"

"You've got to be kidding me."

"I wish I were. There's some maniac running around Staten Island abducting girls and slicing them up. The girls have parents, too. The sooner we get this guy, the safer everyone will be."

Cavanaugh stared at the elevators. He shook his head and started walking back to Stephen's room.

"Well, what do you say, Tom? I need your help."

"Where do you want to meet?"

"Why don't we go back to the restaurant where you were

yesterday? Maybe it will help you remember things."

Cavanaugh checked his watch. "I'll be there in a half hour, but I'll tell you I'm not happy about this."

"I can't remember when you were ever happy. Oh, make sure you bring your brother, too. I want to find out more about the guy he was with."

*   *   *   *

Gretchen gave up screaming for help. No one came and all she got for her efforts was a sore throat. The bright UV lights above her blinded her. She lay on the table sobbing. Where was she? Why was this happening to her? Was this what happened to the other women? She wasn't one for prayer, but she prayed.

The air was hot and humid, yet lying naked on the table she shivered. The sound of the long cylinder against the wall continued. She tried to sleep, but between the constant bubbling sounds and the bright lights, she couldn't.

She squinted to her left and the open eyes of three floating women's heads stared down at her.

Then she heard a noise from the wall in front of her. It sounded like a door was sliding open. She strained to lift her head. There he was. Standing in the same three piece striped suit he wore in the restaurant. He moved quietly like a cat and stood at her feet and smiled.

"Get me out of here!" she screamed.

He smiled and his eyes scanned her body. "You are more beautiful than I expected, Gretchen."

"Why are you doing this?"

"No need to shout, Gretchen. The room is soundproof. No one can hear you." He stroked his hands against her toes. "Are you cold, sweetheart?"

"Stop it!" She struggled against the straps. "Don't touch

me!"

"Relax, Gretchen." His hands moved slowly up her leg. "So smooth. Beautiful. Soft and tender."

"Stop it! Please stop it. Let me go. I won't tell anyone. I promise."

"Oh now, don't lie, Gretchen. We are going to be close – very close!"

He leaned down and stroked her feet. She continued to pull against the straps. The straps cut into her wrists and ankles. Then he reached down and started to suck on her toes. She felt sick to her stomach.

"Stop it! Stop it!" she demanded.

"You are a feisty one, aren't you, Gretchen? I like that."

"Please, I'm begging you."

He stood up and moved his hands up her legs. "You'll get used to me, sweetheart. You have no place to go. Relax."

"Why are you doing this?"

He smiled again and brushed her pubic hair. "I think you are going to need a shave. I'll take care of that later." His hands moved to her breasts and massaged her nipples. Then he stopped. "I'm sorry, Gretchen, but I have to go now. I am really sorry, but trust me, I will be back. Unfortunately, I have some unexpected funeral arrangements to make."

He twisted the ends of his moustache and wiped his mouth. "We have much to talk about." He started to laugh and his laughter echoed throughout the room. "We have much to talk about!" It was a hideous laugh like the cry of a wounded bird. It sent shivers up her spine.

"Why are you doing this?"

His laughter persisted as he backed away. "Because I love it!"

Then he turned abruptly to the floating heads in the jars on the wall. "Will you keep an eye on her, ladies? We don't want her to be lonely. I have some work to do, but I'll be back later to play."

* * * *

When Sgt. Malchus Anthony awoke from a disturbing sleep, he sneaked out of the Chinese Scholar's Garden without noticing the floating body of Jimmy Chen. Anthony's head throbbed and he was sore all over. The dreams last night were disturbingly real. He recalled the dead Viet Cong returning to attack him. He saw the flames from the village leaping into the sky. Their ghosts had come back to get him. He fought them off. It had seemed so real. His body ached from the struggle.

He slipped back through the fence and walked up Bard Avenue. At a bagel store on Forest Avenue, he took the last of the tip money he had stolen from the restaurant and bought a bacon and egg on an everything bagel. On the way out of the store, he poured himself a vanilla bean coffee and left without paying for it.

He headed back to the supermarket where Jack Bennis had found him. When he got there, he folded his legs beneath him to pretend he had lost his legs and used his now empty coffee for donations.

An elderly lady with bluish hair and a shopping cart looked down at him. "Glory be to God, what happened to you?"

He stared up at her. "I stepped on a land-mine in Vietnam. I lost both legs."

"No. I mean your face. It's bleeding."

Anthony reached up and felt the blood. "Some kids beat me up last night and stole my money. God forgive them."

The woman opened her purse and dropped a ten dollar bill in his cup.

"Thank you, madam. God bless you." He smiled through blackened lips. Sgt. Malchus Anthony knew how to survive. He survived in the jungles. He would survive on the streets of New York.

* * * *

Walking into The Waterview Restaurant, Jack Bennis and his brother were involved in an animated discussion. Tom Cavanaugh shook his head. "This is all your fault! I should be with Fran and Stephen now."

"My fault? What are you talking about, Thomas? It's your friend who called us down here."

"If that girl hadn't recognized you, none of this would have happened."

"Oh now I suppose I'm responsible for her going missing."

A tall man with gray hair and a goatee and moustache approached them with his hands straight out in front of him. "Excuse me, gentlemen. Please keep your voices down. This is a restaurant, not a football stadium."

Cavanaugh brushed the man's arms away. "And who the hell are you? The librarian?"

The man lowered his voice and his arms. "I'm Alan Nilsen. I own this restaurant and if you two have a beef, you can leave now and take it outside."

Bennis stepped forward and extended his hand. "I'm Father Jack Bennis and this is my brother. I apologize for any disturbance we may have caused. We were discussing your waitress who went missing last night."

Cavanaugh took a deep breath. "We're supposed to meet a Detective Morton Goldberg here."

Nilsen relaxed his shoulders. "Yes. He's expecting you. He's inside at the table in the back by the window. You can't miss him. He's the one wearing a yamika."

Cavanaugh poked his head into the restaurant. "Yep! That's him."

"Please keep your voices down."

"We will, Mr. Nilsen. Thank you," Fr. Bennis promised.

Goldberg was watching two tug boats escorting a large container ship up the Kill van Kull towards the Howland Hook Marine Terminal.

"OK, Morty, let's cut to the chase. What's so important to drag me away from my son in the hospital to see your sorry face?"

Goldberg rose. "It's good to see you, too, Tom. I see you're still the same *meshuggener* you always were."

"What can we do for you, Detective Goldberg?" Fr. Bennis said extending his hand.

"It's good to see you again, Father. Please have a seat. I just have a few questions to ask you."

Goldberg explained how he was assigned to help in the investigation of the murders of the two women whose severed bodies had recently been found. Mayor Don Juliano and Police Commissioner Arthur Forster wanted the killer captured quickly and quietly, but facts about the murders leaked out, and the press declared there was a serial killer on the loose and named the killer "the Staten Island Butcher" causing widespread panic. The situation was exacerbated when Sophia Bellini went missing. That was when Goldberg was ordered in to work the case.

"The waitress who served you both yesterday was Gretchen Leone. Her grandmother called the precinct this morning to report her granddaughter never came home last night. In view of the circumstances, I didn't want to wait the usual twenty-four hours so I decided to look into her missing immediately on the chance the cases may be connected."

"Sounds reasonable," Cavanaugh said, "but why call us

in? We really don't know what happened to her."

"Well, the truth is Ms. Leone was very excited about seeing her former English teacher here and learning he was actually a priest."

Bennis smiled. "She was a good student. I hope to God nothing has happened to her. How can we help?"

"First, I have to ask you who the old soldier was who was with you?"

"His name is Malchus Anthony. I met him once when I was at Ft. Benning. It was a long time ago."

"How did you happen to get together with him yesterday?"

"My brother met him lying in the doorway of a supermarket on Forest Avenue and decided to do the *Christian thing* and take him to dinner."

"He recognized me, Detective. I don't know how. It was so long ago. We met in a bar and there was a lot of drinking going on. To be honest, I'm not too clear about what happened that night."

"The guy probably saw you were good for a free meal. Let's face it, Jack, the guy is a taker. And I told you, he's a pervert, too!"

Goldberg leaned forward and frowned, "What do you mean, Tom?"

"Well, where do I start? How about he's a homeless alcoholic with obvious psychological problems?"

"Hold on, Thomas. That's not quite fair. Sgt. Anthony suffered a lot of trauma in the war."

"He was in Vietnam, Jack! That war has been over for a long time. He was part of the Mai Lai massacre. Whatever trauma he has, he deserves it!"

Goldberg's head moved from brother to brother as if he were at a tennis match.

"He was part of the Mai Lai massacre. They killed men,

women and children. They burned their homes, raped women, poisoned their water supply, and slaughtered their livestock. He was a murderer! And, if you ask me, he still is a murderer!"

"You weren't there, Thomas. You have no idea what happened or how it affected the soldiers who were there."

"You're incorrigible, Jack. How do you explain his so called black handkerchief? Face it. Your friend is a pervert!"

"Hold on a second," Goldberg interjected. "What's with this black handkerchief and his being a pervert?"

Fr. Bennis stared out the window, stroked a small scar on his forehead, and remained silent.

An attractive waitress with short black hair and a safety pin through her left eyebrow came over to their table carrying three heavy menus. "Hello. My name is Kathy. I will be your waitress this afternoon. Would you like to order a drink, gentlemen?"

Goldberg glanced at Cavanaugh and Bennis. "You must be Kathy Flynn. You called in sick last night, didn't you, Ms. Flynn?"

Kathy's face turned red. "I... I ...."

Goldberg showed her his badge. "No problem, Kathy. I would just like to ask you a few questions about Gretchen Leone before we leave. I'll just have coffee."

"Make mine black, no sugar," Cavanaugh said.

Fr. Bennis looked up. "I'll have the same, thank you."

"Would you like to order something now or would you prefer to wait?"

"Just coffee," Goldberg said and as Kathy backed away he turned to Cavanaugh. "What's the deal with the old soldier's black handkerchief?"

"It was a pair of woman's undies. I didn't like the way he wiped his nose with it. I also didn't like the way he gawked at our waitress. It was like he was undressing her with his eyes."

Goldberg scribbled some notes as he continued questioning the brothers. "Did this Sgt. Anthony make any sexual remarks to Ms. Leone?"

"I told you, Morty; he practically undressed her with his eyes. He was staring so hard at her boobs that he knocked over the salt and pepper shakers when reaching for bread."

"Wait a second, Thomas. He wasn't the only one staring at her. What about that guy in the table in front of us? The one who ordered two white wines. I saw him staring, too."

"You saw him, too?"

"I'm not blind."

"Sometimes you could fool me."

Goldberg held up his hands. "Hold on, guys. One thing at a time. Where can I find this Sgt. Anthony?"

"I have no idea, Detective. I saw him panhandling at the supermarket on Forest Avenue. But he's homeless and there's no telling where he is now."

"You might try the homeless shelters, Morty, but he didn't strike me as the kind that would go to one of them."

Kathy brought their coffees and backed away quickly.

"Okay. Now what about that other guy?"

"Well," Fr. Bennis began, "he was well dressed and ...."

"Hold on, Jack. What can you tell us about the dead women found in the lakes?"

"I can't tell you anything."

"Two can play that game. I know you didn't give the press everything. What else can you tell us? Come on, Morty, I worked with you for a lot of years. Whatever you tell me will stay here."

Goldberg took a sip of coffee and shook his head. "I knew this was a mistake talking to you. You're right. We haven't told the press everything. If we did there would be mass hysteria. The bodies showed signs of pre-mortem bruising indicating the killer possibly tortured his victims before killing them. The bodies we found were cut up as the press indicated, but what they don't know is the hands and heads of the victims were cut off, too."

"He's keeping them as trophies!"

"That's what we think. We can't identify the bodies as we have no fingerprints and no dental records. Whoever the killer is, he is skillful with the knife. We think he knows a lot about the anatomy. He could be a doctor or a surgeon or a medical student."

Cavanaugh and Bennis looked at each other, but said nothing.

"Okay. I told you all we have. We haven't found Sophia Bellini or Gretchen Leone. We're hoping he's keeping them somewhere and hasn't harmed them, but that hope is slim. Now what about that other man who was staring at Gretchen?"

"He was wearing a dark three-piece herringbone suit. He had black hair slicked straight back and one of those Salvador Dali moustaches."

"Do you know his name?"

Fr. Bennis replied, "No. But I think I've seen him somewhere before. I just can't remember where."

Goldberg finished his coffee and started to get up. "Thanks for everything. I appreciate your help. If you think of anything else, give me a call."

"Wait a second, Morty. Before you go, I heard on the radio that there was another body found floating in the Koi pond at the Chinese Garden. Do you think this is the same guy?"

"No. Not unless he changed his MO. The victim was an Asian male and his neck was broken. We think he might have put up a struggle with his killer. Forensics is checking for possible DNA."

"You'll keep us informed, won't you, Morty?"

"No!" Goldberg stood and shook their hands. "Remember, what I told you is confidential."

"Where do you think you're going?" Cavanaugh asked. "Who do you think is going to pay for the coffees?"

"I'll pay for them as long as you both promise to stay away from this case."

Cavanaugh and Bennis looked at each other and smiled. "Never mind. We'll pay for them ourselves."

Goldberg closed his eyes and shook his head. "I knew this was going to be a mistake talking to the both of you. When am I ever going to learn?"

* * * *

Cavanaugh and Bennis watched Detective Goldberg move to the bar and start to question the bartender. Alan Nilsen hovered behind him like a home plate umpire checking for spitballs. Larry Green, the restaurant manager, peeked out of the kitchen. Jack Bennis turned away and rubbed the small scar on his forehead.

"Never play poker, Jack."

"What?"

"You're too easy to read. You have a giveaway 'tell.' Whenever you stroke that scar over your eye, I know you are nervous and thinking of something. Right now, I think you're thinking of getting involved in Gretchen's disappearance."

Bennis dropped his hand and clutched his coffee cup. "She was one of my students, Thomas. She was a good kid. I feel responsible."

"You're not responsible, Jack. Bad things happen to good people. You know that. Nobody ever said life was going to be fair. It is what it is."

Bennis stared down at his empty coffee cup.

"Okay, brother, I know that look. What are you planning to do and how can I help you?"

"You've got enough to worry about what with Stephen in the hospital. It's just that I don't think Sgt. Anthony is the killer they're looking for. From what Goldberg told us the killer is meticulous, careful, and skillful. Anthony doesn't fit that profile. Besides, he would need a place to keep these women. It would be pretty difficult for a homeless alcoholic to do this."

"You know my feelings about the sergeant, Jack. Presuming you are right – which I have serious misgivings about – what can you do?"

The priest remained silent for a few minutes and then looked back at his brother. "You go back to the hospital. Stay with Fran and Stephen. I think I'll pay a visit to Gretchen's grandmother. She could use some comfort."

Cavanaugh signaled the waitress over. "Okay, big brother, do your priest thing. I've got the check."

Bennis rose slowly and smiled. "You know, Thomas, you're not that hard to read either. I see that look in your eyes. What are you planning?"

"I'm not sure. But I do miss the hunt. Maybe there is something I can do." He grinned the mischievous smile of a ten year old. "Just say a prayer that we both don't get caught up in something we can't control."

Bennis nodded, "Amen to that."

*   *   *   *

Otto Grub liked to work alone. It was less complicated and his "little secret hobby," as he called it, was safer that way. The murder of Jimmy Chen, however, threw a wrinkle into his plans. Now, he would have to hire some of his on-call workers. Now, he would have to worry about someone discovering his "projects" in his private room in the basement. Now, he would have to tolerate potentially inquisitive visitors to his home.

He cursed under his breath as he looked at the phone on his desk and thought of the series of calls he would have to make. In his mind's eye, the image of Gretchen lying naked on one of his special tables floated in and out.

"Concentrate, Otto!" Suadela ordered over his shoulder. "You have a job to do. One thing at a time. She will wait."

He took a deep breath. "You're right, Suadela."

"I always am. Now make your calls!"

He called Jimmy Chen's father from his office. Otto took meticulous notes as he always did. Mr. Chen knew what he wanted. Although he would not come to the funeral home, he would send his daughter with a picture of Jimmy and a biography to place in the newspaper and on a card for visitors. She would pick out the casket for her brother.

Grub stared at a reproduction of Mia Tavonati's painting of "Metamorphosis" on the wall and wondered what Mr. Chen's daughter looked like. "Concentrate, asshole!" Suadela chided him. "You have Gretchen. There's no need for another – at least not at this time."

He picked up the phone and continued with his calls. Jimmy Chen's body would be released from the morgue the next day. He knew from experience autopsies are best performed quickly before organs begin to deteriorate. Autopsies themselves typically took only about two to four hours. The police would receive a preliminary one-page report within twenty-four hours. The full report including toxicology tests would come up to six weeks later. Jimmy's sister would sign a release form and Grub would pick up the body in the morning.

He wondered who killed Jimmy Chen. Whoever it was had complicated his plans. Suadela was right about the

Chinese Scholar's Garden being close to the spot where he captured his latest toy. Had someone seen him?

He clasped his hands. They were cold. He checked his rolodex. He called Cathy DeGaetano and Liz Castro, both licensed embalmers. They would prepare Jimmy's body for viewing. They were professional, dependable, and discrete. They knew enough not to ask questions.

He hesitated when arranging for pallbearers. He frequently hired retired cops, but he didn't want additional police hovering around the funeral home. "Call them," Suadela ordered. "There always will be police watching the funeral of a murder victim. Using ex-cops will deflate the situation. They will be grateful for the job and help in controlling any boisterous visitors and press that may come."

Otto Grub checked his list and called four retired cops: Paul Scamardella, Mike Marotta, Steve Impellizzieri, and Dennis Coppolino. He had used the four before. They were big, strong, unintimidated Italians who followed orders and would mind their own business.

When he finished with his calls and secured the necessary help, he leaned back in his chair and ran his hands through his jet black hair. Then a buzzer startled him. He had a visitor at the front door. For an instant, he froze. "Could this be the police?"

"Snap out of it, asshole. You're going to blow this whole thing if you don't get control of yourself!"

He turned and looked up at her. "But who would it be, Suadela?"

"How about getting off your ass and going to see for yourself? It's probably Jimmy Chen's sister. Isn't she supposed to bring you materials and pick out a casket for her brother?"

Grub checked the clock on the wall. "Yes, yes, of course, that is probably who it is."

"Don't try anything with her. People know she came here."

He turned back to Suadela. "Thank you. I don't know what I'd do without you."

"Shut up and get the door. I'll be downstairs watching your latest prize."

* * * *

Driving along Forest Avenue on his way to the hospital, Cavanaugh saw Sgt. Anthony begging across the street in front of a Stop & Shop. Traffic was heavy. He pulled over to the curb and rolled down his window. "Hey, Sarge, remember me? My brother took you to lunch yesterday."

Anthony unwound himself and stood up quickly. The elderly woman who had given him money came out of the supermarket as he was getting up. "You have legs!" she shouted. "You're a fraud!"

Anthony emptied his coffee cup with money into his pocket and reached into the woman's shopping basket and pulled out a package of cookies.

"Help! Help!" the woman screamed.

As Cavanaugh started to get out of the car, he saw Anthony push the woman down and grab her purse. The woman flew back against shopping carts crying.

Anthony turned toward Cavanaugh and warned, "Stay away from me!"

Cavanaugh got a good look at the bloody scratches on the sergeant's face. He dodged cars and trucks trying to get across the street. When he finally did, however, Anthony had jumped the fence in the back of the store and disappeared into the woods. The woman lay crying beside her overturned basket. Her head was bleeding and she kept sobbing softly, "Why did he do this? Why?"

Cavanaugh knelt by the woman and took a clean

handkerchief and applied pressure to her cut. He then dialed 911 and waited with the woman till help arrived.

When an ambulance arrived, Cavanaugh dialed Goldberg's number. "Morty, I just saw Malchus Anthony, the soldier my brother met yesterday at The Waterview Restaurant. He knocked an old woman down and stole her purse. He had scratches on his face."

"Where is he now?"

"He got away. He jumped a fence in the back of the store and disappeared into the trees."

"Stay away from him, Tom. He's dangerous. We just got a match on the fingerprints found on an empty bottle of Wild Irish Rose in the Chinese Scholar's Garden. They are his. The scratches on his face were probably from his struggle with Jimmy Chen. We'll know when the final reports come in, but I think we have enough now to arrest him."

"Do you think he murdered those girls, too?"

"I don't know, Tom, but knowing how the system works they will probably try to pin them on him, too. If those black panties he has match up with the DNA of one of the women, I think it will be a slam dunk."

"But where would he keep those girls? And how would he manage to slice them up like you said? The way I saw his hands shaking at lunch, I doubt he'd be able to carve a turkey."

"That's above my pay grade. I'll let the prosecutor deal with that. Thanks for the tip. We'll cover that area with a fine tooth comb. He won't get away."

Cavanaugh watched the ambulance take the woman away. He looked into the woods behind the store. Somehow he doubted the police would find him. Anthony had survived the jungles of Vietnam. The more he stared into the trees, the more he began to think that his brother might be right about Anthony not killing those women. But if he didn't, who did? And how would they find the so-called Staten Island Butcher?

* * * *

When Otto Grub opened the front door of the Grub Funeral Home, he looked down at a petite Asian woman in a sleek, tight-fitting black dress. He scrutinized her dark downward slanted eyes, her long flowing black hair, and her pale skin. Her dress hugged her lean body and conveyed both modesty and seduction.

"Good afternoon, Mr. Grub. My name is Kim Daggett. I am Jimmy Chen's sister."

"Daggett?" Grub asked holding the heavy door half open.

Kim bowed politely. "Yes. Daggett is my married name. My husband is a New York City policeman. Jimmy is my brother. My father sent me here."

Grub's hand on the door shook. If Chen's brother-in-law is a cop that would mean more cops would be at the funeral. He wanted to run away to his special room in the basement.

"May I come in, Mr. Grub, to discuss Jimmy's funeral?"

"Oh, yes. Forgive me. I was thinking about something else."

He escorted Mrs. Daggett into his office where they discussed funeral arrangements. Her father would not be attending the wake and funeral. She gave him pictures of Jimmy and a brief biography. She briefly explained some of the traditions in her family and how she was bound to abide by her parents' requests. "I do not necessarily believe all of my father's beliefs, Mr. Grub, but out of respect, I obey his decisions."

She presented him with a handwritten list from her father. It included all the details he wanted for his son's funeral. Kim Daggett emphasized the importance that all the procedures her father listed be followed in a proper and dignified way. She emphasized that her father believed any irregularities could bring bad luck and tragedy to their family. "My father is not exactly religious, but he believes in certain traditional Chinese customs. He believes it is important to pay reverence to the dead, for the dead can influence the house of the living and bring bad luck on to their descendants."

Otto breathed a silent sigh of relief when he learned her father did not wish a colorful, elaborate funeral ritual and procession. He nodded approval when told Mr. Chen did not want any religious service. For some reason, Otto and Suadela always felt uncomfortable around religious services.

After arrangements had been agreed upon for a three day wake, Otto Grub and Mrs. Daggett took the elevator to the third floor display room. Here he showed her an assortment of overpriced caskets and urns. He knew some Chinese families preferred the traditional irregular hexagonal shaped timber Asian coffin with sides that taper from top to bottom which he did not have on display. "If you wish, Mrs. Daggett, I could order a special casket, but it might take a day or two days."

"That won't be necessary. My father is not a rich man, nor a very religious man. He chooses to follow most, but not all, family traditions."

"I understand," Grub said and started to explain the special features of the caskets on display.

"That won't be necessary. My father will not be attending the funeral. He gave me authority to choose the casket of my choice. Let's keep it simple. A plain pine coffin will be sufficient and less costly."

"But, Mrs. Daggett, ..."

Jimmy Chen's sister folded her arms. "My decision is

final, Mr. Grub. Are there any additional papers I need to sign?"

Looking at Kim Daggett standing in front of a mahogany casket in her tight-fitting, black *qipao* with her long flowing black hair and captivating dark eyes, Otto Grub felt the urge to take her right there. He envisioned lifting her into the casket and having sex with her on the white velvet lining. He started to move toward her.

Mrs. Daggett stood still and nodded at him. "If there is nothing else, Mr. Grub, I must be going. My husband is waiting for me in his car outside."

His body shook and he backed away. "Of course. No. You have signed all the papers necessary. I will prepare the obituary notices and distribute them to the newspapers and take care of the rest of the arrangements. I will pick up your brother's body and we will prepare it for viewing as soon as possible."

Grub's hand was shaking when he pressed the elevator button to go down. Suadela was right. He could hear her chastising him about his having both a penis and a brain, but not enough blood supply to run both at the same time. He was becoming careless. He still had Gretchen in the basement. He would have to be more careful over the next few days.

* * * *

Greta Johnson was pouring a cup of tea when the doorbell rang. Her heart skipped a beat. She dropped the kettle and boiling water spilt over the countertop. She stood still. Was this the news she dreaded hearing about her granddaughter? Had the police found her or had the Staten Island Butcher killed her?

The doorbell rang again.

Greta untied her apron, took a deep breath, and brushed her hair back. She said a silent prayer as she opened the door.

"Good morning, Mrs. Johnson. I'm Lucy Bauer from CBS News. What can you tell us about your missing granddaughter?"

Greta's face reddened. She looked at the young red-headed woman in her green cardigan top coat and red, white and blue scarf holding a microphone up to the door. Behind her a heavyset man with a Yankee baseball cap focused a film camera on Greta.

"Please, leave me alone. I have nothing to say to you."

Lucy Bauer put one hand on the door and shoved the microphone at Greta's face. "Have you heard any news about Gretchen? Do you think she's another victim of the Staten Island Butcher?"

"What's wrong with you people?"

The reporter pushed against the door. "Can you describe how you feel? When was the last time you spoke to your granddaughter?"

Greta pressed against the door pinching the reporter's foot.

"Move your foot, lady, or I will call the police. You are trespassing."

Lucy Bauer removed her foot, and Greta slammed the door shut. She leaned against the door and started to sob. Suddenly, there was another knock on the door. She swung the door open and shouted, "I told you to leave me alone! Now go away!"

"I apologize, Mrs. Johnson. I'm Father Jack Bennis. Gretchen was one of my students back at Garfield Academy. She waited on us yesterday at The Waterview Restaurant. I just wanted to convey my condolences and offer to help in any way I can."

Greta blushed. "I'm sorry, Father. I thought you were the reporters again."

"I understand. They have a tough job and can be brutal at times."

Greta Johnson stared at the priest, but said nothing. She felt her heart beating. She held her breath.

"Are you all right, Mrs. Johnson?"

She shook her head. "No. I mean, yes. I'm sorry. It's just.... Would you like to come in?"

The priest followed the grandmother into her living room. There were a variety of pictures hanging from the beige walls and on the mantel. He recognized Gretchen's graduation picture and pictures of Gretchen and her grandmother. There was a picture of a much younger Greta holding a baby and pictures of Greta with a beautiful young woman. He couldn't help but admire the young woman. Then there were pictures of Greta and the young woman holding a baby. He wondered if the young woman was Gretchen's mother.

"Please, have a seat, Father. May I get you a cup of tea?"

"If it's not too much trouble, I'd love a cup of tea."

"I was just brewing it. It will only take a second. Make yourself comfortable."

Fr. Bennis sank down into a colorful sofa and surveyed the room. There were pictures hanging everywhere. Most of them showed Gretchen, Greta, and the young woman. Some captured scenes of sunset on the beach, the Grand Canyon, the Golden Gate Bridge, Wrigley Field, Faneuil Hall, the World Trade Center, and various other points of interest around the country. But one thing struck him. There were no pictures of any men.

When Greta Johnson returned with the tea, Fr. Bennis began the conversation by pointing to the pictures on the wall. "I see you and Gretchen did some traveling."

Greta blushed slightly. "Yes. I tried to take her to various places over the summers. Have you done much travel, Father?"

He rubbed the scar on his forehead. There were so many places, so many countries, and so many violent stories. He sipped his tea and said, "Yes. I have done some travel."

Greta Johnson stared at him. Her hands grew cold. She felt a chill rising up in her chest.

"Gretchen was a good student. It was such a pleasure to talk to her last night. She seemed shocked to see I was a priest."

"She told me about the rumors around the school, but she never believed them. Were you always a priest?"

Bennis smiled. "No. I spent some time in the service before."

"Where were you stationed?"

Bennis rubbed his scar again. "All over. But that was a long time ago. Tell me about your granddaughter." He pointed to one of the pictures on the mantel. "Is that your daughter with Gretchen when she was a baby?"

A solitary tear rolled down Greta's cheek. She wiped a tear from her eye. She looked at the priest and nodded.

"This must be a terrible time for you, Mrs. Johnson. I am truly sorry. Is there anything I can do to help?"

She looked him straight in the eye. Her voice was calm and determined. "You can bring my granddaughter back to me."

Bennis ran his finger over the scar above his eye. "I'm not sure I can do that, Mrs. Johnson, but I will definitely pray for her safe return."

"You said you were in the service."

He took another sip of tea. "Yes, but I'm not a

policeman."

"By any chance were you ever stationed at Ft. Benning in Georgia?"

"Yes, I was, but that doesn't mean I can find your granddaughter. That was a very long time ago."

"Gretchen told me you helped catch that killer who called himself *Lex Talionis*, the man who was killing people at Garfield Academy."

"I worked with my brother back then and we got lucky."

"You were in a special branch of the service, weren't you?"

Bennis straightened his back. Mrs. Johnson continued to stare at him. She didn't seem to blink.

"Well, yes. I was. But how did you know?"

"You went on a number of covert missions back then."

"I don't understand. How did you know?"

"You were a lot younger back then. So was I."

He stared at her. His brow furrowed. His missions were top secret. Who was this woman? How did she know about his service?"

Mrs. Johnson sat in silence. It was as if she were debating something with herself. Then she stood and took a picture from the mantle. "This is a photo taken of my daughter shortly after she had Gretchen."

"She's very beautiful, Mrs. Johnson."

"Her name was Jaqueline. She died a few years ago in a car crash on the Staten Island Expressway."

"I'm so sorry. She was so beautiful."

"It was God's will, Father. I accept that."

They sat in silence for a few minutes. Then Greta Johnson said, "I always loved the name Jaqueline. I named her after her father."

Jack Bennis' eyes jumped from the photo to Mrs. Johnson. Her eyes seemed to burrow into him. He shifted in his seat and handed the picture back to her. "She was truly very beautiful."

"She was in all respects. She was a good mother and a good daughter. Her husband, however, was a bum. She thought she could change him. She couldn't. One day he disappeared with a barmaid and abandoned his wife and his daughter. We never heard from him again. I hope he's dead. The world would be a better place without people like him."

"You obviously did a great job raising Gretchen. I will offer my Masses for her."

"You'll do more than that!"

"Excuse me."

"You'll find my granddaughter and bring her back to me."

"I can't promise that, Mrs. Johnson. It's in God's hands."

"You don't recognize me, do you, Father Bennis?"

The priest frowned. "I'm afraid I don't understand."

"Before you became a priest, you were an officer in a covert group sanctioned by our government to assassinate certain people."

His eyes widened and his mouth dropped.

"I thought it was you, but that scar above your eye convinced me. You got it in the Philippines. It came from a sword called a Ginuntin."

"How…how did you know?"

Greta Johnson lowered her head and studied the photo in her hands. "You really don't recognize me. But why would you? You were so drunk that night."

Bennis sat dumbfounded. He touched the scar on his forehead. "How did you know about the scar? Even my brother doesn't know how I got it."

Greta looked tired. "You told me, Jack."

"What? When? I never met you before."

"We had met in a bar and we ended up in a bed in a motel in Americus, Georgia."

"I'm sorry. I don't remember."

"Maybe part of it was my fault. You were drunk. I never made love to a man before. Even though you were drunk, you were kind and caring and good looking, too. You told me stories of your missions. At times, you cried about what you did."

"I am so sorry."

"Bad things happen, Jack. They are part of life. It's how we handle our problems that matter."

Bennis lowered his head. He wanted to tell her she made a mistake, but he remembered parts of that night in the bar with deer heads mounted on the wall and waking up in the motel room with a terrible headache.

"Why did you leave?"

"You looked so peaceful sleeping there. I knew how much you had been through. You told me things you shouldn't have. I thought you would be embarrassed when you woke up and maybe a little angry. So I folded your clothes and quietly left."

"Why did you fold my clothes?"

"I guess I felt sorry for you. You were like a gentle Teddy bear. You weren't mean or abusive. I hoped we would meet again, but we didn't."

"I shipped out on another assignment the next day. It turned out to be my last mission. I was wounded and left for dead in the jungles of Colombia. I didn't know what happened that night. I swear I didn't know. "

Greta Johnson studied the picture of her daughter and her granddaughter. "And I didn't know until a few months later that I became pregnant that night."

She held out the picture of herself, Jacqueline, and Gretchen. "And that, Jack Bennis, is why you are going to help me find my granddaughter because she is your granddaughter, too."

The Staten Island Butcher

* * * *

III

Kneeling in the chapel at St. Peter's, Jack Bennis prayed harder than he had ever prayed before. Maybe it was a mistake. How did she know all the details of his life? Maybe he did have sex with her that night. Maybe the sweet smell he remembered from the following morning was perfume. Still that didn't mean he was the father of a child he never knew. A paternity test would prove if he were the father or not. But in the photos of Jacqueline he saw his own nose and eyes. He had to find out if it were true. Either way, however, he had to find Gretchen Leone. He couldn't turn away. What if she really was his granddaughter? But how would he find her? Where would he start?

Greta Johnson told him he was the first. The sergeant who was with him paid her and her friends. She never had sex before and didn't again until after she had Jaqueline. Did he believe her? When she left the motel room, she said she checked his wallet. It was empty. But she memorized his name. "You always want to remember your first," she told him, and she wanted to know his name. Was she telling the truth?

When Gretchen brought home stories about her English teacher, she wondered if he could be the same Jack Bennis she made love to in a sleazy Georgia motel room so long ago. She doubted it could be he, but when she saw the scar over his eye, she knew it was. Could Gretchen really be his granddaughter?

Suddenly, his cell phone rang. Was this God speaking to him? No. That would be too simple. It was probably his brother. He checked the number. He didn't recognize it. He stared at the phone and it rang again and again. "Answer it," a voice in his head urged. His hand trembled when he said, "Hello."

"It's me!" a voice responded.

"Who are you?"

"Me. Malchus. I need your help. The fucking cops are after me."

Bennis looked up at the crucifix above the altar.

"Are you fucking there? You've got to help me. I heard the news. They think I'm the fucking Staten Island Butcher."

"Are you?"

"No! I didn't kill nobody! You've got to believe me."

"How can I help you, Malchus? You need to help yourself."

"Yeah, I know. I've heard that before. I know I need help. You're a fucking priest now. Maybe I can meet you somewhere. I really need your help, Jack. I didn't kill those girls!"

"Can you come over to St. Peter's Church? I will wait for you in the chapel. We need to talk."

"Okay. Okay. But no cops. You got to help me. "

The phone went dead. Bennis sat down in the front row and took out the rosary his mother gave him. As he started praying the first Sorrowful Mystery, the Agony in the Garden, his phone rang again. It was his brother.

"Jack, I saw your sergeant friend. He was in front of the Stop & Shop on Forest Avenue. He pushed an old lady down and stole her pocketbook! I was right about him."

"Wait a minute. You saw him?"

"Yeah, and he had scratches on his face. I called Goldberg and he told me they found his fingerprints in the Chinese Garden where that kid was killed last night."

"Where is he now?"

"I don't know. He took off into the woods. Goldberg said they'd cover the area and find him. I'm not so sure. For an old guy, he moved pretty fast, and he's a sneaky son of a bitch. Goldberg told me he's got a record and is dangerous. If he tries to reach you, Jack, call Goldberg right away."

Bennis bit his lip. "Thanks, Thomas. I'll keep an eye out for him." He looked around the chapel. It was empty. "How is Stephen doing?"

"The doctors say he could come home tomorrow."

"That's great news. Tell Fran I love her and will keep praying for all of you."

Bennis hung up and took a deep breath. Was he doing the right thing in not calling the police? Was Sgt. Anthony the Staten Island Butcher? He didn't know. He didn't think so, but he didn't want to think Gretchen was his granddaughter either. Could Anthony help him find Gretchen? He ran his hand over his scar and continued to pray.

* * * *

Gretchen Leone shivered on the metal table in Otto Grub's secret room. The noise from the bubbling machine next to her seemed to grow louder. Between the noise and the lights she could not sleep. She dreaded his return. Her back ached. The leather bonds on her wrists and ankles cut into her skin from her futile struggles to free herself. She lost touch of time. How could she escape this madman? The smell in the room made her nauseous. And now she had to pee.

She heard the door sliding open. He was back. "Help! Help! Please let me go. I'll do anything you want, but please let me go."

"Isn't she beautiful, Suadela? Look at that tattoo of a heart with the initials J. G. inside it. I wonder what his name is."

"Maybe it's not a male. It could be a woman."

His laugh echoed through the room. "That's a good one, Suadela. Wouldn't it be funny if she were a lesbian? Oh, that would be so exciting!"

Gretchen strained to see him. "What are you talking about? Let me go, please! I have to go to the bathroom."

"You look cold, sweetheart. You're shivering."

"Please, I'm begging you." She looked up and saw him smiling at her side. He wore a light blue surgical gown. In his hands he held a can of shaving cream and a razor. "What are you doing?" she cried.

"I told you that you needed a shave. This will make you feel better."

"Get away from me. You are crazy!"

He reached down suddenly and grabbed her hair. "Don't ever say that again!"

She squinted up at him. "What kind of a man, ties a woman down and tortures her? You are a pathetic waste!"

She felt the sharp pain in her head as he pulled on her hair. Then he drove her head back with a tremendous force. As her head crashed into the metal table again and again and again she heard him shout, "I am not a waste of life! I am not a poor excuse for a man!" And then there was only darkness.

*　*　*　*

Cavanaugh and his wife ate a quiet meal in their house. Outside it was raining again and the wind whipped against their windows. "It will be good to sleep in my own bed tonight," Fran said between bites of her favorite broccoli rabe pizza that Cavanaugh ordered. He topped off her glass of Reasons' Cabernet Sauvignon and filled his glass again.

"They were very nice in the hospital, but it's no fun sleeping in a chair every night. I'll be so happy when Stephen comes home tomorrow."

Cavanaugh nodded his head and started reading the *Staten Island Advance*.

"You're not listening to me!"

"What?"

"You keep reading that stupid paper and you haven't heard a word I said."

Cavanaugh looked up. "No, I heard you. I agree. You must have been uncomfortable there. I'm glad he's coming home, too."

"We used to talk about things at dinner, Tom, but now all you do is grunt and read the newspaper."

"It's not that, Fran. The waitress we met yesterday at The Waterview went missing. Goldberg thinks she might have been taken by this guy the papers are calling the Staten Island Butcher."

"Everyone in the hospital was talking about him. People are really worried."

"The guy my brother brought to lunch with us was an old army sergeant. Jack met him when he was in the service. I think he could be the killer. I saw him this afternoon. He grabbed an old lady's pocketbook and ran away."

"Oh, my God! You didn't run after him, did you?"

"No, but I called Goldberg, and he told me they found his

fingerprints in the Chinese Garden where that security guard was killed. They think he's the killer."

Fran sat frozen with a slice of pizza in one hand and her glass of wine in the other.

"I called Jack to tell him. He's been pretty upset about the missing girl. He taught her at Garfield Academy a few years ago. He said he was going to visit her grandmother this afternoon. I told him to notify the police if Sgt. Anthony tried to contact him."

Cavanaugh opened the newspaper to the obituary section.

"You don't think Jack will go after this Sgt. Anthony, do you?"

"You know my brother, Fran. I wouldn't put anything past him. But I don't see how he would find him."

Fran reached for the bottle of wine and poured herself another glass. Cavanaugh buried his head in the newspaper.

"Why do you always check the obituaries?"

"Did you know Benjamin Franklin read the obituary page in bed every morning? He said if his name wasn't in it, he would get up."

"Very funny, but you're no Benjamin Franklin."

"That's true. Sometimes I feel more like Clarence Darrow. He said he never wanted to see anyone die, but sometimes he read the obituaries of certain people with extreme pleasure."

"You are incorrigible, Thomas Cavanaugh."

He smiled and started to read the obituary of Jimmy Chen. "Wow! I didn't realize the murder victim at the Chinese Garden was related to Kim Daggett."

"Who's she?"

"She's the wife of a good friend of mine, Lt. Daggett. We worked together in Brooklyn. Matt loved to tell the story of his great-great-grandfather, John Daggett, who was once the superintendent of the San Francisco Mint back in 1894. According to him, John Daggett had twenty-four special Barber head dimes made, and he gave them to seven of his closest friends, including three to his youngest daughter, Hattie. He knew the dimes would be worth a lot more in the years to come and told Hattie not to spend any of the dimes until she was much older."

"That makes sense. I wonder what those dimes are worth today."

"Brace yourself, Fran, but today an 1894s Barber head dime is worth close to two million dollars!"

"Oh, my God! Does he still have the dimes?"

Cavanaugh smiled. "Well, that's the thing. According to Matt, the guy's daughter went out and spent one of them on ice cream!"

Fran laughed. "That was certainly an expensive ice cream!"

"I think I'll drop by the funeral home tomorrow to pay my respects."

"Find out if he still has any of those dimes left."

Fran and Cavanaugh were laughing when the phone rang. They looked at each other in dead silence. After the second ring, Cavanaugh answered the phone. He listened intently for what seemed like an eternity to Fran. He nodded, "Yes" and "I understand" a number of times. Fran held her breath. A cold chill rose in her chest.

Finally, Cavanaugh said, "Thank you," and hung up. He avoided looking at Fran.

"Well, who was it?"

Cavanaugh took a deep breath. "It was the hospital. There have been some complications...."

"What complications?"

"There were some abnormalities in Stephen's latest EKG. They want to keep him for a few more days."

"Oh, no! I knew this was going to happen. This is just what I was afraid of. He's probably got inflammation of his coronary arteries. I read online how that leads to myocarditis and aneurysms and heart failure. He's going to die, Tom! He's going to die! He's our baby, and he's going to die!" She knocked her half empty glass of wine over and started sobbing.

Cavanaugh jumped up and hugged his wife. He stroked her hair. "They said they wanted to keep him for a few days to monitor things. They are putting him back on aspirin and intravenous gamma globulin to lower the risk of coronary artery problems. He's going to be all right, Fran. Trust me, Fran. He's going to be fine."

Fran buried her head in his arms. She wept quietly, but said nothing.

* * * *

Two candles flickered on the altar as the red sanctuary lamp dangled from the chapel ceiling at St. Peter's. Darkness covered the rest of the chapel. Fr. Bennis heard the door in the back open and the heavy footsteps coming down the aisle. He turned. Sgt. Malchus Anthony stood like a dead tree in the middle of the aisle. Bennis rose and motioned him to a pew in the front.

"Is it safe here?" the sergeant asked.

"This is God's house. You can't get any safer."

Anthony plopped down. His face was lined with bloody scratches. His eyes were glassy. He smelled of cheap alcohol and sweat.

"Where did you get the money for the booze?"

Anthony's head snapped toward him, "What?"

"Did you get it from the old woman you robbed this afternoon?"

"Your brother told you, didn't he?"

"He called it in to the police. They're looking for you."

"No shit, Tracy. I've been avoiding them all day."

"What's the story with you, Malchus? You're a mess. I know veterans often have trouble adjusting to civilian life, but you're a smart guy. Why haven't you sought help?"

"Help? That's a load of bull shit! There's nobody to help."

"What about the Veterans' Administration? They have all sorts of counselling, therapy, and treatments available. You served our country. They're there to help."

"You're fucking naive, Jack. You probably always were. They awarded me a silver star for 'gallantry in action against an enemy of the United States.' I served close to three tours of duty in Vietnam. I saw what happened at Mai Li, but I didn't participate in it. When we moved on to the next village, we took some fire. Some of our men were hit. The officer in charge ordered me to tell my men to kill everyone in sight and to burn their hootches and huts. He was specific. 'Kill all the men, women and children,' he said. 'Let God sought them out!' I refused. I saw what happened at Mai Li. He told me he was giving me a direct order. I couldn't do it, Jack.

"I may be a low life, but the massacre at Mai Li was wrong. I didn't want to have any part of another Mai Li. But he kept insisting he was giving me a direct order. Then he took his .45 out and said if I didn't do what he ordered, he would shoot me dead right there."

Bennis studied his face. Anthony stared at the crucifix hanging over the altar. His hands were clasped tightly together. Was he telling the truth or was this a phantom of his imagination?

"You don't believe me, do you?"

"You claim you didn't participate in the Mai Li massacre?"

"I was delayed at our last outpost. As we were clearing

80

out, we took some rounds from the Commie Gooks. I helped some of the wounded into an evacuation helicopter. I didn't get to Mai Li until early afternoon. Most of the killing was done by then. But I did see them setting fire to their huts and then shooting the women and children as they ran out. There were piles of bodies all over the place. It was fucking sickening. I saw them shoot a grenade launcher into a group of people who were still alive. And I just stood there and watched. I did nothing to stop it. It's haunted me ever since."

"What did you do when your commanding officer ordered you to do the same thing?"

Anthony lowered his eyes. "I made a mistake."

"A mistake?"

"Yeah. I shot the officer in the leg. My mistake was I should have killed the bastard!"

Bennis saw tears in Anthony's eyes. He touched the sergeant's shoulder. "You shot the officer?"

"Fucking-A I did! I should have fragged him, but I didn't. They arrested me and threw me in the brig. They were planning on sending me to Leavenworth. Under Article 90 of the Uniform Code of Military Justice, they can sentence you to death for willfully disobeying a superior commissioned officer in wartime. They would have done that, too, but they were afraid my men would mutiny and the whole story would hit the press. So they stripped me of my medals and gave me a dishonorable discharge."

"Is that why you haven't applied for Veterans' benefits?"

"That's one of the reasons. They don't give benefits to anyone with less than an honorable discharge. I'm *persona non grata* even though I won a silver star, fought almost three full tours in Vietnam, and potentially saved a village from extermination."

Anthony took a breath and turned to Bennis. "The other reason is I don't want to have anything to do with a government that turns its back on its servicemen."

Bennis ran his hand over the scar on his forehead. "Those articles in the Uniform Code of Military Justice pertain to obeying *lawful orders*. An order that is unlawful does not need to be obeyed."

"Tell that to the judge. I shot a fucking officer. Who was going to believe me? What's done is done. If I had it to do all over again, I would have killed the bastard!"

The two men sat silent in the flickering lights of the chapel. Then Fr. Bennis asked, "What happened the other night at the Chinese Garden? The police claim to have found your fingerprints there."

"Yeah. I was there. I stole the tip from a table at the restaurant when I slipped out and I bought a bottle of wine. I must have blacked out."

"Do you remember going to the Scholar's Garden?"

"Yeah. I was there. I found a quiet, dry space out of the rain and finished the bottle of Wild Irish Rose. I remember having another horrible nightmare. Maybe it was from the wine."

"What did you dream?"

"I dreamt the Viet Cong were coming at me. I was scared shitless. I fought one of them off. I think I broke his neck. It seemed almost real. I get the chills now even thinking about it."

"I think your dream was real, Malchus. A security guard was killed that night." Bennis pointed at the sergeant's face. "They think he put up a struggle and scratched his assailant. They will probably find your DNA under his fingerprints."

"Shit! What am I supposed to do now? I didn't mean to kill anyone. I thought it was a bad dream. Now they're going to try to pin all the dead girls on me."

"Maybe I can help you. But you have to be honest with me. My brother told me about the black panties you used as a handkerchief in the restaurant. If they match the DNA from the handkerchief with the DNA of one of the murder victims, they will have a damn good case against you."

"Okay. Okay. You know I'm not a nice guy. But I swear before that God of yours, I didn't hurt any young women."

"You certainly admired our waitress yesterday."

"I'm not dead, Jack. I found those panties in a garbage pail along with a lot of women's clothes. I kept them to remember the way things once were."

"Where did you find them?"

"I don't know. Somewhere along Richmond Terrace, I think."

"If I drive you there, would you remember?"

"Maybe. I don't know." He paused and looked at Bennis. "Are you going to help me or not?"

Jack Bennis leaned closer. "Do you remember anything else about last night?"

"What do you mean? I told you I was drunk."

"I visited the grandmother of the waitress this afternoon. She lives about a mile away from the restaurant. The way I figure it, Gretchen must have walked up Kissel Avenue which is adjacent to the Chinese Scholar's Garden. Did you see or hear anything that night?"

Sgt. Anthony closed his eyes and held his head with both hands. "It's kind of foggy, but I remember squeezing through the gate when I heard a car stop across the street. I was afraid he might have seen me. I ducked behind some bamboo trees and almost lost my booze."

"What did you see?"

"It was dark and raining, and I was drunk. I didn't see much. I heard a man's voice say something. Then a door opened and closed. After the door closed, the car accelerated quickly and fishtailed up the street."

"What kind of car was it?"

"I don't know. It was dark and raining pretty heavy. I think it was black. It was big. I remember that. Maybe it was one of those limos or SUVs or Town cars."

"Good. Now let's get you up to my room. We'll clean up your face and I'll get you some new clothes and something to eat."

"Then what?"

"Then you'll sleep in a bed and in the morning we're going looking for that place where you found the clothes."

"So you'll help me?"

"We'll help each other."

The sergeant rose and gripped the priest's arms. "One more thing, Jack. Do you think you could get me some of that sacramental wine you guys use? You know. Maybe for a little night cap?"

* * * *

Gretchen Leone slowly regained consciousness. Pain throbbed through her head. The dark world seemed to be spinning around her. Where was she? She tried to move her arms, but they were tied down. She began to remember. Fear gripped her. Then she felt it. It was cold and damp. It came from her pubic area. She pulled her head up a little and saw the top of his head between her outstretched legs. He had a safety razor in one hand and a can of shaving cream in the other. The bastard is shaving me, she realized.

He had her securely tied down. She thought of her grandmother's advice. "Never give up, child. *Illegitimi non carborundum* – never let the bastards grind you down!"

Gretchen knew she had to do something. She couldn't let him take advantage of her. She had to retaliate, to put up a fight, even if it were futile. What was it Tennyson said in his poem "Ulysses"? Though much may be taken, much still abides, and though she may have been made weak by time and fate and a sick psychopath, she was still strong in will to strive, to seek, and not to yield.

Gretchen Leone knew he might kill her. No, she knew he was going to kill her sooner or later. It was only a matter of time before she would be another head floating in a jar of formaldehyde on a shelf in his private, soundproof torture chamber.

No, she was not going to yield without a fight. She remembered the story Mr. Bennis told the class about the boy who threw a snow ball at the new limousine and how the driver stopped and pulled him into his car. She smiled through the pain. She knew what she was going to do.

She opened her eyes slightly so she could see his face and then she tightened her muscles, squeezed, and emptied her bladder with all the force she could muster into his face.

* * * *

After a shower and shave, Malchus Anthony looked like a different person. Once he removed the dried blood from his face, the sergeant's swarthy complexion concealed most of the scratches. Still, Fr. Bennis knew the sergeant's distinctive Army field jacket would draw attention to him.

He searched his closet for clothes for him. Partly, out of necessity because he didn't have many civilian clothes, he decided the best he could do was to disguise him as a priest in one of his black cassocks. People rarely look at priests in the street, and if they do, his experience was, they usually nod and then turn away. He picked out a clerical collar and Jesuit cassock with a cincture to be knotted on the right side.

"Are you out of your mind?" Anthony said. "I ain't wearing no woman's dress!"

"It's a cassock, Malchus. I'll be wearing a cassock, too. A

blind man would be able to identify you in that God-forsaken Army field jacket of yours. If you want me to help you and avoid the police, you'll wear it. We will be in the car most of the time anyway."

Anthony sat on the priest's bed. "I don't like it. That's all I'm saying."

"Okay. You said it. Now get to bed."

"Where are you going to sleep?"

"Don't you worry about me. I'll be right here on that futon sofa bed by the door."

Sgt. Anthony looked around the room. There wasn't much furniture in the room – just a plain wooden desk, a chair, a bed and a used black futon convertible lounger. "Why are you doing this?" he asked. "You can get yourself in a lot of trouble."

"Someone once said it's better to give than to receive. I feel good helping you."

"But I'm not a good guy. I probably did kill that kid in the Garden. I stole that old woman's pocketbook and the tip from the table in the restaurant."

"You also broke into the poor boxes in the church."

"How did you know that?"

"The video cameras caught you in the act."

Anthony shook his head. "Why are you continuing to help me?"

"Nobody's perfect, Malchus. I believe Jesus died for all our sins, and He taught us to love one another as He has loved us. Look at it this way, He's my commanding officer, and He's asking me to do the right thing. I'm trying to do that. And hopefully, we'll both help each other in finding our missing waitress."

"I don't know how good I'm going to be. Sometimes I feel like that fucking scorpion who talked the turtle into letting him ride on his back across the water after promising he wouldn't bite him. When they were half-way there, the scorpion bit the turtle in the head. The turtle turned and asked him why the fuck he did that. Now both of them were going to die. His answer was, 'That's my nature.' I don't know how good I'm going to be, Jack, but I'll try."

"Good. That's all anyone can ask. This is a long shot anyway. Now let's get some sleep. We are going to have a busy day tomorrow."

"What about the money I stole?"

"I already emptied it from your jacket while you were in the shower. If you need it back, just ask for it."

"But what do we do when they see me on the cameras?"

"The pastor already reported it to the police. When they see it's you, hopefully it will distract them for a while so we can do some reconaissance work of our own looking for the place you found those women's clothes."

Sgt. Anthony scratched his head and looked up at the priest. "You know you're a crazy bastard."

"Yes. My brother tells me that all the time."

*   *   *   *

IV

Fran and Tom Cavanaugh spent the night in their son Stephen's hospital room. Various doctors and nurses occasionally came in to check the monitors attached to Stephen. Each one assured the parents the child was going to be fine and that they should both go home and get some rest. They refused. At 3:00 a.m., Cavanaugh's head jerked and he came out of a light sleep. Beside him Fran slept with an open copy of *Good Housekeeping* in her lap. He sat for a long while in the semi-darkness of the room watching Fran, Stephen, and the monitors. In the corridor outside the room, he saw a nurse either checking a patient's chart or reading what he thought might be a romance novel. He couldn't be sure, but then he noticed her head occasionally bobbing up and down. She was nodding off.

He stood and walked around the room. They didn't both need to be here. He walked out into the corridor. The nurse's head jumped up. One of her hands covered something she was reading. "Is everything all right, Mr. Cavanaugh?" she asked brushing her hair back with the other hand. He tried to see what she was reading, but she leaned over and covered whatever it was.

He wanted to grab her hands and see what she was reading. He wanted to tell her to get off her ass and check on the patients. He wanted to remind her of her duties. But he took a deep breath and said, "Fine. I'm just going for a cup of coffee. May I get one for you, too?"

The nurse blushed, and she smiled. "I don't think the cafeteria is open now, but there is a coffee machine on the third floor."

"How do you like your coffee?"

"Regular with two sugars, if you can."

He took the elevator down. The hospital was quiet, eerily quiet. He knew there were doctors, nurses, aides working, but where were they? The noise from the coffee machine broke the silence. He heard coughing in one room. A male nurse sat behind the nurses' station on the third floor. He checked Cavanaugh, nodded, and went back to whatever it was he was doing.

He brought two coffees and one tea back with him. When the elevator opened on Stephen's floor, he saw the nurse talking to a young man who, in Cavanaugh's eyes, could have been a high school student, an aide, or a nurse. He gave the nurse her coffee and discovered the young man was actually an intern. Getting old sucks, he thought. Kids are running the world now. Where had all that time gone?

Fran looked up when he entered Stephen's room. He kissed her on the forehead and gave her the tea. "Where were you?" she asked.

"I was falling asleep. You were out cold and Stephen was sleeping. I thought I'd get some coffee."

"It seems so quiet here."

"It wasn't that way in the emergency room. Some poor guy came in who was having a heart attack. The doctor told him he was going to die unless he had a heart transplant right away. Just then another doctor runs in and says, 'You're in luck! Two hearts just became available so you can choose which one you want.' It turns out one belonged to a lawyer and the other to a social worker. The poor guy was clutching his chest and couldn't make a decision so he asked me for advice."

Fran sipped her tea and smiled. "And what did you supposedly say?"

"I told him to take the lawyer's."

"Why?"

"Come on, Fran. It's a no brainer. Everyone knows that social workers are bleeding hearts and the lawyer probably never used his."

"You're incorrigible, Tom," she whispered.

"Yeah. I think it runs in the family."

He sat down next to her and held her hand. He looked at Stephen and then Fran. "Seriously, I can't just sit around here. I'm bored stiff."

"Somebody's got to stay with him. I don't want him waking up and finding no one here."

"There's no reason for both of us to stay with him. Why don't we take turns? You go home now and get some rest. I'll stay here until you come back."

Fran checked Stephen. "I don't know. Someone should be here for Stephen."

"I'll be here. You go home, get some rest and then come back in the afternoon. I'm reading this book *Operatives, Spies, and Saboteurs.* It's about some of the untold stories of the OSS in World War II. Some of the stories are fascinating. Did you know Julia Child worked for the OSS on inventing some kind of shark repellent?"

Fran rolled her eyes. "My sister is supposed to come by later."

"Good. When you come back, I'll go home and maybe

drop off at the funeral home and pay my respects to Lt. Daggett's brother-in-law."

"Are you sure, it's okay?"

Cavanaugh reached down and pulled his wife up. He hugged her and gave her a long kiss. "I love you, kid," he whispered in her ear.

Suddenly, they heard a soft cough at the door. They turned. It was Nurse Palladino again. "I'm back," she smiled, "and I thought I told you two to cut out the fooling around. This is a hospital, not the back row of the movie theatre."

* * * *

V

Otto Grub woke up with a start from a deep sleep. Suadela stood above him glaring down at him. "Are you a complete idiot?" she shouted.

He sat up and rubbed his eyes. "What are you talking about? What did I do now?"

"It's your precious Gretchen with the cute tattoos in your 'play room'! If you don't take better care of her she's going to die!"

"She's going to die anyway. They all do. You know that. That bitch pissed in my face. What did you expect me to do?"

"You almost beat her to death! You can't keep them tied down without food or water. The wake upstairs is going to keep you busy for a few days. If she dies, there will be no more hunting for you until Jimmy Chen is buried. You know how you get when you have no 'toy' to play with."

"What am I supposed to do?"

"Treat her better if you want her to last. Give her some food and water. The basement is going to stink for days if she gets sick and you don't clean it up."

"And how am I going to do that? What if she escapes?"

"Use your head, asshole. Handcuff her to something down there. Show her what happens when they don't obey you. Show her Sophia Bellini. She should be ready by now. When she sees what happens when they fight you, she'll come around."

Otto looked at his hands. His knuckles were scraped and bloody. His shoulders ached from the beating he gave Gretchen. He admired Suadela. "You are beautiful and right once again. What would I do without you?"

"Get up now. You have a lot to do. You need to pick up Jimmy Chen's body at the morgue and give instructions to your morticians and your security people. Flowers will start arriving. What time are the men coming?"

"I told them to get here by 10:00. But what about Gretchen?"

"She's still breathing. You need to go down there now while she's still unconscious and secure her to something secure. Then you can wash her and bring her some food and water. Kindness is a gift the deaf can hear and the blind can see. As the saying goes, 'You catch more flies with honey than with vinegar.' Give it a little time. If that doesn't work, then, of course, you can kill her."

* * * *

Father Bennis and Sgt. Anthony drove up and down Richmond Terrace for two hours looking for the place Anthony said he found the women's clothes. The sun shone down on the Bayonne Bridge. Construction vehicles, delivery trucks, and potholes forced them to travel slowly. "Does anything look familiar?" Bennis asked.

"I don't know. I think I found them in a garbage can by a

store."

"A store?"

"Yeah. I think it may have been a grocery store. I was hoping there might be some food there. I lifted the lid and there I found the clothes."

Bennis turned around at Port Ivory and slowly retraced their route. This time he was looking for a grocery store.

"What kind of clothes were they?"

"Hell, I didn't look that close. I took the panties. I think there was a red shirt, a pair of stiletto shoes, a pair of sneakers, a couple of bras...."

"A couple of bras?"

"Yeah. They were different, too. I remember that. One was like a 4X wireless job with pink lace along the top. The other was much smaller. It was like a simple blue padded double A bra. It had a cute little bow in the middle. They were definitely from two different people."

"What else was there?"

"I was looking for food. Under the clothes I found a couple of stale Devil Dogs. That's about it. I took the panties and the Devil Dogs."

Bennis knew it was a long shot. This was a real "Hail Mary." His chances of finding the store were slim. Even if he did, whoever put them there probably just dropped them off. He wouldn't be so careless to leave them in his own garbage. But it was all he had to go on to find Gretchen.

"There it is!" Anthony shouted. "That bodega on the corner! I remember it now. I got the panties from their garbage."

Bennis turned up the street and circled the block. He checked the houses. There was a furniture restoration store, a hardware store, a string of townhouses, an abandoned factory, a funeral home, a paint store, a fish and bait store, a CVS, a nail salon, a bar, and some single family homes.

"Now what? Do we start knocking on doors and asking who left the clothes?"

"No. We are going to need help on this."

"I got an idea, Jack. Why don't we just visit the bodega and get something to eat. All this driving around's made me hungry."

* * * *

When Otto Grub arrived at his funeral home with Jimmy Chen's body, Paul Scamardella, Mike Marotta, Steve Impellizzieri, and Dennis Coppolino were there waiting. They each wore a dark black suit. Otto prided himself on his attention to details and had picked up a dozen assorted donuts and a jug of coffee from Dunkin' Donuts for the ex-cops. As he handed out the donuts, he gave each an assignment. Scamardella would be in charge of flower arrangements. Marotta and Coppolino were to take the body to the preparation room where Cathy DeGaetano and Liz Castro would work their cosmetic magic. Impellizzieri's job was to pick up materials from the printer. He emphasized to each man the need for efficiency and speed. After their initial assignments, they were to rotate shifts to ensure no visitors came in until the morticians released the body for viewing. Then they were there to maintain order. Because the first viewing would take place that evening, he wanted them to control any crowds that might come. Under no circumstances were any visitors to have access to the elevator.

"Do you expect a large crowd?" Marotta asked.

"I want to be prepared. The deceased was a college student, and he was murdered. In addition to family, there may be classmates, neighbors, friends of the family, the press, and, of course, the curious."

Coppolino complained, "I don't think you'll need us the whole night. I wanted to go home early to watch 'Dancing with the Stars.'"

"Tape it. I need you here. If you can't handle it, I'll get someone else."

When they all agreed, they helped take Jimmy Chen's body from Grub's Cadillac Escalade ESV and went about their assigned duties.

Suadela appeared in the garage doorway. "Good work, Otto. It looks like you're finally getting some balls. I see you cleaned up Gretchen and left food and water for her."

"I think I'll go visit her now while I have some free time."

"What did you do with her clothes?"

"I took care of them."

"That's not what I asked. I hope you didn't dump them in the garbage like the others. That was careless. It could come back to bite you in the ass."

"Don't worry. I burned them in the fireplace. There's no way I can be connected to the disappearances."

"Good. We wouldn't want a stupid mistake to destroy our little game, would we?"

Grub smiled. "I think it's time to show Gretchen what happened to Sophia. This should be fun!"

"It will be a thrill to see the look on her face."

Grub started to laugh a high pitched laugh that sounded more like screeching. "Yes! Yes!" he cackled rubbing his hands together as he walked toward his elevator. "Yes, it will be such fun!"

* * * *

Fran's sister arrived at the hospital around 10:00. Cavanaugh waited until Fran arrived and then went straight home. He checked the mail. There were the usual cruise brochures, an offer to join a gym, a political survey, bills from National Grid, and VISA, and two personal letters. Both letters came from Colombia, South America, and were addressed to his brother.

He studied the letters for a few minutes. One came from Bogatá and the other from Cartagena. One was typed and the other handwritten. He placed the mail on the dining room table and went upstairs to shower and shave.

When he came back downstairs, he checked the letters again and decided to call his brother.

* * * *

Fr. Bennis and Sgt. Anthony walked into the bodega on Richmond Terrace in their clerical cassocks. A thin Hispanic man with gray hair and deep-set sad eyes stood behind the counter eyeing them. There were two aisles crammed with canned food, condiments, detergents, and cookies. On one wall a refrigerator displayed sodas, beer, milk, and juices. Behind the counter, there was a small coffee machine and another refrigerator unit that held various cheeses and cold cuts.

Bennis asked, "Could you fix us a couple of sandwiches, *por favor*?"

"*Sí*, Padre. What would you like?"

Anthony spoke first. "How about roast beef and American cheese on a roll with plenty of mayonnaise?"

Bennis's cell phone rang. "I'll have the same, but make mine with mustard, please." He looked at his phone and then turned to Anthony. "It's my brother. I'll take it outside."

Anthony nodded and as the man started to prepare the sandwiches, he wandered down one of the aisles. The store was neat and clean. Everything was lined up evenly. A small bell announced a young man with a hoodie who came in as

Fr. Bennis left. The man behind the counter turned. "Not now," he said.

"The man sent me here to collect. You're a week late, Carlos."

"Now is not a good time. I have customers."

The hooded man looked around. Anthony was in the aisle by the beer and sodas and could not be seen. "I don't give a shit who you have here. I came to collect."

"Let me make them their sandwiches and then we can talk."

"Time's up, Carlos. No more talking." He pulled a miniature baseball bat from his pocket. "Give me the cash now!"

Carlos froze. His fingers were in the midst of cutting the roast beef. The man with the hood reached over and grabbed Carlos's hand. "I got a job to do, Carlos. This is business." He reached back with the bat when a voice behind him said, "I don't think you want to do that."

Hooded man turned and looked at Sgt. Anthony in his black cassock. "Mind your own business, Father."

"The man's making me a sandwich. Put the bat down."

"Beat it, Father. This ain't none of your business."

Anthony moved from the shadows of the aisle toward the hooded man. "It is my business. He's making me a sandwich."

The man with the bat stared at Anthony. The sergeant moved closer.

"Go away, old man! Go back to your prayers before you get hurt!"

"Maybe you didn't hear me, kid. I told you to put the fucking bat down. Now do it before I get angry."

The hooded man let go of Carlos's hand and turned toward Anthony. "You don't know who you're talking to, old man."

Anthony grabbed the bat with one hand and squeezed his throat with the other. The man's hood fell back as Anthony lifted him up and threw him into the neatly lined food cans. He took the bat and started to beat him over his back and head.

"Stop! Stop!" Carlos threw his arms up and pleaded. "*No más*! You're going to kill him!"

The bell sounded again as Fr. Bennis rushed back into the store with his cell phone still in his hand. Cans were crashing down around him. He grabbed Anthony and pulled him away. "We've got to get out of here, Malchus. I'll have to call you back, Thomas."

Anthony stood with the bloody bat in his hand. "But, Jack, we haven't gotten our sandwiches yet."

A voice from the cell phone asked, "What's happening? Jack, are you with Anthony? What the hell is happening?"

"Long story. Talk to you later." Bennis hung up, dropped a twenty dollar bill on the counter, pulled Anthony over the limp, bloody body of the now hoodless man and pushed the sergeant into his car.

* * * *

Detective Morty Goldberg sat at a temporary desk set up for him at the 120 Precinct. Next to him were two college students mulling over printouts of the texts Gretchen Leone received and sent on the night of her disappearance. He specifically chose to call Joel Littman and Jeannie Covino down to the station to help decipher the messages and to give him more information about those who sent the messages. Joel was Gretchen's boyfriend, and Jeannie was her best friend. If anyone could give him a better idea of the message meanings, he figured, they could.

Joel was a 6'7" forward on Wagner College's basketball

team. He scored 24 points in a loss to Iona College the night of Gretchen's disappearance. Jeannie and Gretchen were best friends from kindergarten. Jeannie was majoring in criminal justice and law enforcement at St. John's University and in the midst of rehearsals for an upcoming production of *The Little House of Horrors*. Neither knew anything about what happened to Gretchen and were both upset. They studied the messages intently.

Jeannie looked up from the text messages. "I really don't like doing this, Detective. I feel like I'm prying into Gretchen's private life. They are just normal messages. You know who sent them, why don't you just ask them?"

"I hoped you could give me an idea of the people who sent the messages. You probably know them all."

Joel pointed to one. "This one is from Vito. He's a good friend, but a real cynic. I think '*bm&y ficcl*' means 'between me and you frankly I could care less.' I think Mr. Bennis failed him."

"Andy sent '*uhgtbsm he a priest?*' I think it means, 'You've got to be shitting me. He's a priest?'"

Goldberg pointed to "*ILUWYWHXOXOXO*." "This one is from you, Joel. What does that mean?"

Joel blushed. "It means, 'I love you. Wish you were here....'"

"I sent 'TTUL'," Jeannie said. "It means 'talk to you later.' My boyfriend Bobby sent 'HFAC' meaning 'Holy flying animal crackers!' He thinks he's funny. He was with me, Gracelyn and Judy Vernon at rehearsals. They couldn't believe Mr. Bennis was really a priest."

"I think Regina may have sent ...."

There was a short knock on the door, and P.O. Cackowski stuck her head into the room. "Excuse me, Detective Goldberg, but we just had a report of a 0403, aggravated assault incident, in a bodega in Mariners Harbor.

I thought you might be interested in it."

Goldberg frowned. He didn't like being interrupted while conducting interviews. He snapped at Cackowski, "I'm not here to handle assault complaints."

"The report is about two priests who beat up a teenager in the bodega."

Goldberg looked confused.

"Their names were Jack and Malchus."

"Malchus?"

"Yes. You were looking for a suspect named Malchus. I thought you might want to know. It's not a very common name."

Goldberg put his pencil down. Malchus Anthony dressed as a priest? Could Jack be Fr. Jack Bennis, Cavanaugh's brother? Was Bennis helping Anthony? He scratched his head. Why had he involved them? He knew something like this was liable to happen. So much for their promises about not getting involved!

* * * *

"What the hell happened in there, Malchus? I leave you for one freaking minute and you end up beating a guy with a bat."

"Jack, you're a priest. You shouldn't be using such language."

"How about I drop you off at the police station and let you explain everything to them?"

"All right! All right! Some guy came in as you left and was shaking down the guy who was making our fucking sandwiches. He was about to hit the guy with the bat when I stepped in."

"Stepped in? You nearly killed the guy!"

"Okay, okay. Maybe I got a little carried away. He called

me an old guy and fucking threatened me! I was just trying to help."

Bennis drove straight down Richmond Terrace. He turned right under the Bayonne Bridge onto St. John Street and pulled over to the curb.

"What are you doing, Jack?"

"I'm thinking of dropping you off here and washing my hands of you."

"No. You can't do that. They'll arrest me."

Bennis checked his rearview mirror. "The problem is now I am involved, too. You're wearing my cassock if you haven't noticed."

"I'm sorry about that. I didn't mean to get you involved. I didn't kill those girls."

"Well, you did get me involved, but the truth is I was involved already. Your black lace handkerchief may have given us a clue. The problem is where do we go now? We can't go back to St. Peter's. They'll be looking for us there."

"You know, Jack, I know it's a bad time to bring this up, but I'm still hungry."

"Shut up and let me think!" Bennis rubbed the scar on his forehead. "We could go to my brother's house, but I don't want to get him involved. He's got enough problems of his own right now."

Sgt. Anthony started to unbutton his black cassock. "Why don't you just let me off here? I'll be fine."

Bennis started the car as his cell phone started ringing. "You're staying with me. I think I'm going to need you."

"Where are we going?"

"Relax. I've got an idea."

His cell phone continued ringing.

"Aren't you going to get that damn thing? It's driving me fucking crazy."

"Let it ring. It's my brother. I'm not ready to talk to him

just yet."

* * * *

Cavanaugh was in the hospital corridor talking to his brother on his cell phone when the line suddenly went dead. He tried calling back, but there was no answer. What had happened? Did he hear his brother say, "We've got to get out of here, Malchus"? Was he with the homeless, alcoholic, pervert Sgt. Anthony? Why would he be with him? Why was there a panic in his brother's voice?

He tried repeatedly to call back, but the only response he got was, "Your call has been forwarded to an automated voice messaging system."

He walked slowly back into his son Stephen's hospital room. His wife Fran's sister, Susan, sat in a chair close to the bed reading *The Little Engine That Could* to his son. He came over to Stephen's bed and placed his hands on the guard rail. He felt his eyes watering as he looked at his little son. The doctors said Stephen was responding to treatment.

"I think I can. I think I can," Susan read aloud.

Stephen's eyes were listless. There was still some purple red discoloration and swelling on his palms. He wondered if Stephen understood anything his aunt was reading. He looked so weak, so helpless. Cavanaugh reached over and patted his son's head.

"Thanks for coming, Susan. It means a lot having you here."

"He's my nephew, Tom, and my godchild. A pack of wild horses couldn't keep me away."

Cavanaugh checked his watch. "What time did Fran say she would get here?"

"Do you have someplace better you have to be?"

"No. It's complicated."

Susan closed the book. Stephen was asleep. "What's so complicated?"

"It's a long story. I was just talking with my brother when something happened. I haven't been able to get in touch with him again. I keep trying, but my calls keep going to voicemail."

"Maybe he's just out of cell phone range."

"No. It sounded like a fight was going on. Then he yelled something and said he'd call me back. I think he's in some kind of trouble."

"You worry too much, Tom. Why don't you just leave? I'm here. I'll stay with Stephen until Fran comes."

He checked his watch again. "No, Susan. Jack's a big boy. He should be able to take care of himself. My place is here. I want Stephen to know his father loves him."

"I think he already knows that."

"I hope so."

"You better believe he knows so," a voice came from the hallway.

He turned to see Fran at the door. She held two large shopping bags. "How is he?" she asked.

Cavanaugh turned and gave her a hug. "The doctors said he's better. They have scheduled him for another echocardiogram in a little while." He paused and pointed at the shopping bags. "Where were you?"

Fran smiled. "I did a little retail therapy. Now you can go to your friend's wake."

"It's my friend's brother-in-law and I don't really need to go. Are you going to be all right if I do go?"

"Of course, I am. Susan and I have a lot to talk about. Now go unless you want to sit here and hear the latest gossip."

Cavanaugh kissed his wife and leaned down and touched Stephen's forehead. "I love you, killer. Be good for your mother," he whispered.

His thoughts shifted quickly to his brother as he walked toward the elevators. Then his phone rang again. His heart skipped a beat. He thought it was his brother, but when he read the caller's name on his cell phone, he felt a cold chill in his chest. The call was from Detective Goldberg.

* * * *

It didn't happen all at once. Gretchen Leone slowly became aware that something was different. She was no longer strapped to a table. A soft white taffeta and lace lining covered her body. Her left hand was handcuffed to an iron pole in the corner of the room, but her right hand was free. Her body ached when she tried to move. Despite the pain, she welcomed being able to move more freely. She tried to stretch. A jug of water and a plate with jelly donuts were by her feet.

She felt it first. A dark figure loomed over her. "It's good to see you are awake, Gretchen."

She looked up at him. He wore a black three-piece suit and was stroking his moustache.

"Why are you doing this? Please, let me go."

He leered at her. "I hope I have made you more comfortable. Your actions upset me greatly, Gretchen, and I apologize for possibly overreacting. Suadela convinced me that we need to cooperate with each other. I have placed some food and water there for you. I hope we can continue our relationship in a more pleasant way."

"What relationship? We have no relationship! You kidnapped me! Now please let me go. Why are you doing this to me?"

"You are truly beautiful, Gretchen. I love the curvature of your body and the softness of your skin. We will have so much fun together."

Otto Grub knelt down next to her and handed her a jelly donut as he stroked her leg. He closed his eyes and murmured, "So soft, so smooth…"

Gretchen kicked the donut out of his hand. "Get away from me, you creep! Don't touch me!"

Grub pulled back as the donut caromed off the machine and splattered jelly on his suit. "I so wish you hadn't done that. I want to be your friend. If you cooperate, things will be a lot better."

"I'm never going to cooperate with you. You are a sick pervert!"

He stood abruptly. His eyes narrowed on her. Then he moved to a switch on the wall and the bubbling noise from the cylindrical machine against the wall stopped. He took a white handkerchief from his pocket and tried to wipe the jelly from his jacket as he walked back to her. "I really hoped it would not come to this. Do you remember hearing about that missing runner, Sophia Bellini? She was nowhere nearly as well-developed as you, my dear."

"What did you do with her? They are going to find you."

"No. And they are never going to find her body either."

Gretchen pulled herself into the fetal position and pulled the lining tighter around her. "What did you do with her?"

He laughed again and pointed to the shelves on the opposite wall. "That's Sophia's head on the right." Then he moved to the machine and turned a lever. Gretchen heard what seemed like the draining cycle of a washing machine. When the machine stopped, he spread his arms and said, "And this, my dear sweetheart, is the fate that awaits you if you continue to fight me like she did."

"They are going to find you. You won't get away with this!"

"But I will. I built this machine myself. It uses a chemical process known as alkaline hydrolysis. It is the latest thing in the disposal of human remains. Isn't it beautiful? It is not yet legal in this state, but the process is simple. I simply mix about 5% of potassium hydroxide with normal water and heat it for a period of time. The body's flesh and organs are dissolved and all you have left is a brittle skeleton."

Grub opened the long cylindrical machine, and Gretchen looked at the white headless skeletal remains of Sophia Bellini. She watched in horror as he scraped the bones out of the machine and placed them in another smaller machine which ground the bones into fine, soft, white dust-like ash.

"This is really so much nicer, don't you think? It beats cutting the bodies up and dumping them in the water. It's so much neater. Right now Sophia's soft tissue has been broken down into a greenish-brown, non-toxic liquid of amino acids, peptides, sugars and salts and is flowing peacefully into our sewer system. They call the process Bio Cremation or Resomation. Once the public gets over its squeamishness and the lawyers, politicians, and religious leaders finally agree on it, Bio Cremation will become the rage. All the tree-huggers will embrace it because it cuts down on carbon dioxide and other pollutants resulting from traditional cremation by fire. It uses much less energy. It's clean and green. And it makes it so much easier to dispose of bodies." He started laughing again sending shivers through Gretchen.

"Look at it, Gretchen. You are looking at the future. You are looking at the cutting edge of cremation. It is already legalized in some states." He patted the long cylindrical machine. "I built this one myself. I admit it is a primitive model, but it does the job, and I am proud of it. I kept Sophia in there longer than a legalized Bio Cremation machine would require, but, as you can see, it works perfectly. The cremulator, which grinds up the bones, only arrived yesterday." He held the fine powdery remains in his hands.

"Look at this, Gretchen. It's almost like dust."

"And what are you going to do with it? Hopefully, choke on it and die!"

"Aha, that's the beauty. It will go beneath the bunting in Jimmy Chen's coffin and be buried with him. No one will ever find Sophia Bellini's body."

He looked over at his display of severed heads bobbing in jars of formaldehyde. "But her head will remain with me forever. As yours will too, if you don't cooperate with my desires. Think it over, Gretchen. I must go upstairs now. Our guests will be arriving soon. Think it over carefully, sweetheart. Sophia was a feisty bitch, and you saw what happened to her. Rest assured, when all our visitors have departed, like General MacArthur, I will return."

* * * *

Cavanaugh waited until he got home to return Goldberg's call. In the interim he called his brother five times. Each time the call went to the automated messaging system. And each time it did, he felt his blood pressure rising. What happened? Why had Jack ended the call abruptly? Why could he not reach his brother? How was Malchus involved in this?

After he showered, shaved, and put some clean clothes on, he fixed himself a grilled cheese sandwich and called Goldberg. "Where the hell have you been?" Goldberg demanded. "I've been trying to get you all afternoon."

"I was at the hospital, Morty. What's so important?"

"Where is your brother?"

"How the hell should I know? I've called him a few times and my calls all go into his messaging system. What's so important?"

"I suppose you're going to tell me you don't know

anything."

"*Au contraire*, my Jewish friend. I know a lot, but I have no freaking idea where Jack is. To be honest, I'm getting a little nervous about it."

"I suppose you know nothing about the assault in the bodega in Mariners Harbor."

Cavanaugh felt his chest tighten. "No. What happened? I've been in the hospital all day."

"I'm sorry. How is Stephen doing?"

"He's scheduled for a few more tests today, but he seems to be doing better. What's with the bodega and my brother?"

"We got a 911 call there was an assault in a bodega. A teenage wannabe was beaten severely with a bat. The owner said two priests were involved."

"Two priests?"

"That's what he said. They were both dressed in black cassocks and Roman collars. The one who beat the kid was called Malchus. The other one was called Jack."

"Oh, shit! You don't think ...."

"What do you think I think? Of course, it's your brother and his soldier friend. Anthony is probably wearing a cassock of your brother's. You guys promised me you wouldn't get involved, and now your brother is an accessory to an assault and aiding and abetting a probable killer."

"No. This is crazy. Jack wouldn't do this. There has to be some reason behind this."

"Do you mind telling me, Tom, what the reason is? I like your brother and can't understand why he would involve himself with Anthony."

"Are you sure it was Anthony?"

"The prints on the bat match his. He's the one who beat the kid senseless. The kid is in critical condition in the hospital now."

The brief conversation Cavanaugh had with his brother flashed through his mind. Why had Jack decided to help Anthony? What happened in the bodega and where were the both of them now?

"Honestly, Morty, I have no idea where Jack is now. I have tried calling him all afternoon, but, as I said, my calls went straight to his messaging service. I was just getting ready to go to the wake for the Chen kid who was killed at the Chinese Scholar's Garden when you called."

"Hold on, Tom. You told me you weren't going to get involved in this investigation. You promised."

"Actually, neither of us promised. If you remember, we picked up the check in the restaurant. But don't get your balls in an uproar. I'm not going there to get involved in anything. I'm just going to pay my respects. Do you remember Matt Daggett from the 5th Precinct?"

"Yeah, sure. He was one of the good guys. I think he was dating some girl named Kim from Chinatown. I read where he made lieutenant."

"It turns out he married that girl, and her brother is your murder victim, Jimmy Chen."

"Well, isn't that interesting? Maybe I'll see you there tonight."

"Not if I see you first."

"Just please don't do anything stupid, *meshuggener*. And if you hear from your brother, give me a call."

Cavanaugh crossed his fingers and promised. Before leaving for the wake, he tried his brother's number once more, but received no answer.

* * * *

VI

The flowers started arriving early. They came from all over New York. There were huge standing sprays of white roses, Asiatic lilies, chrysanthemums, and mini-carnations; sympathy baskets of gladiolus, mums and carnations; bouquets of white roses with Bella Donna Delphinium and blue hydrangeas; floral wreaths of irises, orchids, Michaelmas daises and white poppies. There was a blue and white casket spray of white roses, a delicate purple orchid on a miniature bamboo stalk surrounded by yellow and white chrysanthemums, and even a Chinese paper lantern centerpiece.

Paul Scamardella was a big man to begin with, but since his retirement, he put on close to thirty-five additional pounds. As a police officer, he had worked his entire career in what is known as Manhattan's Flower District. He remembered chasing guys through small jungles of towering green vegetation packed so tightly together you almost needed a machete to get through them. It appeared logical that he would be assigned to handle floral arrangements, except for one thing – Scamardella hated flowers.

His specific instructions were to sign for the flowers and take them up to the viewing area himself. Grub's rules were strict – no deliveries were allowed to be taken to the viewing room except by Scamardella himself.

He followed the rules because the money was good, and it was all "off the books." But as the deliveries started backing up, his back began to ache, and he started sneezing. He knew he was allergic to some kind of flower. He didn't know what the particular flower was, but as the predominantly white and yellow flowers arrived, his sneezing told him that that particular flower had also arrived.

Because Grub locked down the elevators, Scamardella had to lug the arrangements upstairs by himself. After a few dozen trips, he wondered how much more his back could take.

As he tripped and sneezed carrying a large standing spray of yellow and blue chrysanthemums in the shape of a water pipe, Steve Impellizzieri leaned against a side wall and laughed. "You need to lose some weight, Paulie. You're really out of shape."

"Listen, Steve, how about we switch for a while? My back is killing me."

"Are you kidding me? It's good exercise, Paulie. I wouldn't want to deprive you of the chance to shed a few ugly pounds."

Scamardella placed the spray next to the coffin and muttered, "Screw you, too."

Impellizzieri folded his arms and chuckled.

Scamardella was out of breath. He checked Jimmy Chen in the casket and asked, "When are they letting visitors in?"

Impellizzieri checked his watch. "In about another hour. Maybe a little earlier. I hear the line outside is getting long and it looks like snow. The kid must have had a lot of friends."

"That's something you sure won't have." He looked closer at the open casket. "I think you better get Grub."

"Why?"

"It looks like the dead guy's not dead. He's sweating."

*　*　*　*

A light snow began to fall as Father Bennis and Sgt. Anthony pulled up to the curb of a tree lined street. "It's kinda early for snow, ain't it?" Anthony asked.

Bennis didn't answer. His eyes were fixed on a single family white Cape Cod house bordered by a white picket fence. Had it not been for two large oak trees that cast dark shadows on the house, with the snow clinging to the grass, it could have been a Christmas postcard image.

"Where the hell are we, Jack? I'm fucking starving."

"Will you please give it a break? The police are looking for you for murder."

"Why are we here?" Malchus Anthony followed Bennis' eyes. "Do you know someone here? Maybe we can get some food?"

"Knock it off! I'm trying to help you and all you keep doing is complaining about everything. Do you ever think of anyone besides yourself?"

Anthony's eyes narrowed. "I've been around a long time, Jack. Don't try to bullshit me. You're not doing this just for me. What's in it for you?"

Bennis opened the gate without responding. He motioned for Anthony to follow. They cut across the lawn leaving two distinct sets of footprints in the light covering snow. Bennis hesitated at the plain green door.

"I always wanted to know what's behind the green door." Anthony laughed.

The door opened slowly and a woman looked up at them. Her eyes were swollen. Holding one hand on the door, she glanced at both men and then directed her question to Father Bennis. "Did you find her?"

"May we come in?"

"Did you find her?"

"Not yet, but I think we're getting closer."

"How about letting us in, lady? It's freaking cold out here, and it's freaking snowing. Do you have anything to eat? I'm as hungry as a starving cannibal trapped in a van of coconuts."

The woman straightened her shoulders and glared at Bennis. "I asked you to find our granddaughter and you bring me this low life scumbag?"

"Hey, watch who you're calling a scumbag, lady!"

Jack Bennis put his arm out to hold Anthony back. "Can we please come in? We have some things to discuss if we are going to hopefully find Gretchen."

"You're always welcome, Jack, but Malchus Anthony can rot in hell before I let him into my house!"

"Hey, lady, how the hell do you know my name?"

"I never forget a face. In your case, I only wish I could."

"Bull shit! I don't know you from shit."

"The name is Greta Johnson. You raped my best friend and left her for dead in a pile of liquid manure slurry along Pine Tree Road in Georgia."

"Oh, wow! I think I remember her. She was a real blonde as I recall." He smiled. "Yeah, I remember her. You got a good memory. That was a long, long time ago. I think her name was Nancy or Maggie or something like that. She put up quite a fight."

Jack Bennis took a step back and shook his head. He moved his left leg forward, twisted at the waist, and sent a crushing right cross into Anthony's jaw. Anthony's head snapped back, his legs buckled, and he collapsed unconscious into the snow. Bennis rubbed his fist. "Can we come in now, Greta? We really need to talk."

* * * *

Gretchen Leone huddled next to Grub's still warm homemade Bio Cremation machine. How could someone design a machine like this to dispose of bodies? Sophia Bellini was now a pile of fine white dust. What makes someone capture women, torture them, and then kill them?

She looked around the room. Next to the skull, three bobbing heads stared down at her as mute witnesses to Grub's sadistic insanity. Was she doomed to their same fate? She heard her grandmother's voice in her head. "Never give up. Never surrender. Rise up against the odds. Never give up and feel sorry for yourself. If one way doesn't work, find another way."

How could she get away from him? On a shelf under the decapitated heads, she saw a compressor, an airbrush hose, what looked like a makeup case, and a collection of chemicals, solvents, and bleaches. On a gurney, just out of reach, she could see tubing, forceps, needles, hooks, clamps, scissors, and a scalpel.

If somehow she could get free and grab the scalpel, she had a chance. Maybe resisting him the way she had wasn't the best way. She felt her swollen lips. One of her eyes was swollen shut. She tasted blood in her mouth. Her whole body ached. There were bruises on her arms and chest. She felt like her ribs were broken. She pulled the lining tighter around her. What could she do?

She planned to major in theater. She loved acting. Perhaps, if she played him, he would let his guard down and she could reach the scalpel.

But he disgusted her. Every time he touched her she felt like vomiting. The way he twirled his mustache made her want to pull it off his face. How could she avoid recoiling at his touch? But if she didn't, he would kill her. Was she willing to sacrifice her principles? What good are your principles when you are dead?

Gretchen squinted at the floating heads. How had they reacted to him? Even if she did cooperate with him, she knew he was going to kill her. She fantasized that someone would come to rescue her. She closed her one good eye and pictured Mr. Bennis smashing through the door and saving her. She welcomed the fantasy of her old English teacher rushing to her rescue. But then she remembered, Mr. Bennis was a priest, and she started praying as she had never prayed before. No one was going to come to rescue her. No one knew where she was. Perhaps, prayer was her only hope.

*   *   *   *

Jack Bennis felt negotiating with the Iranians on a nuclear arms treaty must have been easier than convincing Greta Johnson to allow Sgt. Anthony into her house. But after he dragged Anthony into her house, he still had to convince her to allow him to stay there while he organized another part of his plan.

Greta folded her arms and looked down at the unconscious Anthony. "You can't be serious, Jack!"

"But I am, Greta. It's our only choice. I can't take him with me. He's like a lightning rod. If the police spot him, we'll both be locked up, and time is of the essence if we're going to find Gretchen."

"But he's an animal. After what he's done, I want the police to lock him up and throw the key away. He deserves to die in the electric chair as far as I'm concerned."

Bennis knelt down and checked Anthony's jaw. "I hit him pretty hard. I hope I didn't break his jaw."

"I wish you did more than that. You don't know what he's done. He didn't even know her name. Barbara was my best friend. He raped her and left her on a pile of manure. Barbara and I went to school together. She could have died there. I don't think she'll ever be the same. It's not fair that he got away with it and you're protecting him."

He looked up at Greta. "I understand how you feel, but we need him."

She shouted at him, "You have no idea how I feel! I want that man dead. I want him to pay for what he did to Barbara!"

"Listen, right now we don't have time to discuss the qualities of mercy and justice. Someone once wrote how the wheels of God grind slowly, but they do grind exceedingly fine. I'm not excusing any of his actions, but I am not his judge. How about a compromise? I'll tie him up until I get back. Then we talk. We need his cooperation, Greta. He may have seen the car that took Gretchen. With his information I think we can find her. We need him. Believe me, I wouldn't ask you this if we didn't need him to get Gretchen."

Reluctantly, Greta agreed, and together they tied Malchus Anthony up with rope, zip ties, and tape and locked him in the hall closet. Then Bennis made a call on his cell phone.

*　*　*　*

Cavanaugh stopped at the florist to get a bouquet of red carnations for Jimmy Chen's wake. As he was waiting, his cell phone rang. It was his brother. "Jack, where the hell have you been? I've been trying to reach you. What the hell happened in that bodega? Are you all right? Is Anthony with you?"

"Hold on, Thomas. Where are you now?"

"I'm at the florist getting some flowers to bring to Jimmy Chen's family."

"Jimmy Chen? Wasn't he the kid who was killed at the Chinese Garden? Why are you going there?"

"I worked with his brother-in-law back in the day. I'm just going to pay my respects. Your bosom buddy Anthony killed the kid."

"Allegedly killed him."

"He did it, Jack, and you know it. Why are you protecting him? The police found his prints in the Chinese Garden and on the bat he used to beat that kid in Mariners Harbor. And, according to my sources, you were with him at the bodega. What's the story? They're looking for you now as an accessory."

"Where is the funeral home?"

"It's Grub's Funeral Home off Richmond Terrace in Mariners Harbor."

"Do you think Goldberg will be there?"

"He told me he would. Why?"

"I've got to meet you. I have something I want you to give to Goldberg. Can you meet me at the Fed Ex building under the Bayonne Bridge in a half hour?"

"What are you up to, Jack? Goldberg is thinking of locking you up with Anthony. He told you not to get involved."

"It's a long story, Thomas, but I am involved. With Anthony's help I'm trying to locate Gretchen Leone, and I think we might have come up with a clue."

"Give it to the police. You're a God-damn priest, not a cop!"

"That's why I want to give you something for them to

check. It's important, Thomas. I wouldn't involve you if I had somewhere else to go. If we are going to save Gretchen we have to act fast. It may even be too late."

"Why don't you just give it to him yourself?"

"The short answer is there will be a lot of formal questions and he'll probably lock me and Anthony up. There's no time to waste."

"Okay. I'll meet you at the Fed Ex building."

"Come alone. No police."

"Okay. I get it. What is this so important thing you are giving me?"

"I want Goldberg to run a DNA test against the bodies found in the lakes and Sophia Bellini's. If I'm right, there will be a match."

"And what exactly are you giving me?"

"The black lace panties Anthony used as a handkerchief."

*   *   *   *

Otto Grub studied Jimmy Chen's corpse. Moisture was on his hands and face. "It's like I told you, Mr. Grub, the dead guy's sweating. I think he's still alive," Impellizzieri said standing against the wall of the viewing room. "Now what the hell do we do?"

"He's not alive. It would be a miracle if he were. His blood has been replaced with formaldehyde during the embalming process. Believe me, Impellizzieri, he's as dead as dead can be."

Impellizzieri started chewing his fingertips. "Then why is he sweating?"

Grub removed a handkerchief from his pocket and dabbed it on Jimmy Chen's forehead and hands. "He's not sweating. He's defrosting."

"Defrosting?"

Grub turned and walked to Impellizzieri. "The Chen family wanted the viewing to take place tonight and tomorrow. I tried to get them to postpone the viewing. I only picked the body up at the morgue this morning. It had been in their freezer overnight. Someone obviously had the temperature too low. A frozen body takes time to defrost. We didn't have that luxury in this case. The moisture you see is a result of the freezing process in the morgue. This happens sometimes. There is nothing to worry about."

"People are going to freak out when they see him sweating. What am I supposed to tell them?"

"Nothing. I will turn the air conditioner on, adjust the lighting, and use a bit of cosmetics to cover the moisture. Some makeup and power applied to the face and hands and no one will know."

As he turned to go to his office, Grub cautioned Impellizzeri. "Make sure no one comes in here until I get back."

When he arrived at his office, Grub saw Suadela sitting at his desk. "Well, now you've done it. You couldn't wait to get back to your precious little Gretchen in the basement and have your fun with her. You rushed things, and now the corpse is sweating! You are a fool, a complete asshole! I don't know how you would exist without my help! How many times do I have to tell you to be more careful? When are you going to listen to me?"

Grub put his hands to his head. "I am listening, Suadela. I am listening. Please, stop yelling at me! I can't stand it when you get angry!"

She pointed to the cosmetic case on the bookcase by the door. "Take it and go fix up the corpse. You need to hurry. It is almost time to let the mourners in. The family will be here soon."

"Please, don't be angry with me, Suadela."
"Go now. I will be downstairs with Gretchen."
"Thank you," he said grabbing the cosmetic case and rushing back to the viewing room.

* * * *

Cavanaugh parked in a spot by the Fed Ex building on Richmond Terrace under the Bayonne Bridge. He held his cell phone in his hand as he looked around. His brother was always meddling in crime investigations. Somehow he always got himself involved. How many times had Cavanaugh told him, "You're a priest, Jack, not a cop"? This case was serious. A young man had been murdered in the Chinese Scholar's Garden. Sgt. Anthony's fingerprints were found at the scene. The way Anthony looked at the missing waitress and the black panties he used as a handkerchief made him the chief suspect in the murder of Jimmy Chen and the disappearance of two women and the murders of two additional women. Why was his brother helping Anthony? He was there when Anthony beat the kid in the bodega half to death. And yet he was still with him.

Cavanaugh looked at his watch and then his cell phone. Should he call Goldberg? Could he get his brother out of this situation before it was too late? Or was it too late already?

But Jack Bennis was his brother. He had to stand up for him. Brothers looked out for one another. Jack had been willing to put his life on the line for him a number of times. If Cavanaugh called Goldberg, a group of squad cars would descend on him like starving piranhas on a dead cow. Jack would be arrested. Anthony would be arrested. What if Anthony didn't kill those women? Cavanaugh knew how the system worked. The mayor and the police commissioner wanted the serial murderer caught. Anthony was the perfect suspect. How would a homeless, alcoholic disgraced veteran defend himself?

His brother did have some valid points. Where would Anthony keep the women? He was homeless. How would he be able to meticulously dissect the bodies found in the water? Anthony's hands shook drinking a glass of water. With a good lawyer, Anthony might be able to beat the charges. But what about his brother? Jack knowingly helped Anthony. He was an accomplice. The press would have a ball publicizing a Catholic priest's complicity in helping a murder suspect avoid being arrested.

He checked his watch and his phone again. When he looked up, he saw a figure walking down the dimly lit road through the fluttering snow. He turned on his windshield wipers. It looked like a woman. As she approached his car, she stopped and peered into his window. Then she knocked gently on his window.

"Go away," he said. "I'm not interested."

Her scarf was wrapped around her face. She leaned in closer. "Are you Cavanaugh?"

"Do I know you?"

"No, but I was told to give you something." She reached into her pocket as Cavanaugh reached for his gun. "Easy, cowboy," she said. "Some priest told me to give you this." She handed him a plastic bag and started to walk away.

"Hold on!" Cavanaugh shouted. "Who gave you this?"

"Some guy like I told you. He said he was a priest and gave me two twenties to give it to you. I did. Now I'm gone."

"Wait a second. How can I get ahold of that guy?"

The woman pointed under the bridge. "He's the guy in the car across the street."

Cavanaugh turned and saw his brother wave at him and then pull away and disappear up St. John's Street. He pounded the steering wheel with both hands. "The bastard didn't trust me!" he hollered. When he turned to look at the woman, she too was gone leaving only faint footprints in the snow.

* * * *

VII

The snow began to fall a little heavier when Kim and Matt Daggett pulled up to the Grub Funeral Home. They could see a line of young people waiting for the doors to open while a number of presumably wiser people remained in their cars. Kim Daggett carried a large box with her. As they approached the main entrance, Lt. Daggett recognized former police officers Marotta and Coppolino standing guard.

"Good evening, gentlemen," the lieutenant said.

"Lt. Daggett," Coppolino said, "are you here on police business?"

He introduced them to his wife and said, "No. I kind of wish I were. Jimmy Chen is my wife's brother."

"I'm sorry to hear that," Marotta said. "Our sincere condolences."

"Can we get inside? We need to set a few things up before the visitors come in."

"Sure thing, sir. Just tell Impellizzieri when you're ready, and he'll notify us to let the people in."

"Impellizzieri? Steve Impellizzieri? He used to work in my

precinct. Wasn't he the one who had his hair styled in some fancy place in the East Village?"

Both Marotta and Coppolino laughed. "Not anymore. He's bald now."

Lt. Daggett shrugged, "I hear that's the new style now."

As the Daggetts entered the funeral home, Otto Grub bowed in greeting, "I hope you will find everything satisfactory." Kim clutched the box she brought close to her breast and said, "My parents will not be coming, Mr. Grub, as I told you. I would like to distribute these gifts to any visitors. Invitations have been sent to family and friends. We expect a larger number of visitors tomorrow."

Grub bowed again and led them into the viewing room. Jimmy Chen's was the only wake being held at the funeral home. A large portrait of Jimmy rested in front of a massive display of flowers. Jimmy's body was in a full length open casket.

Kim Daggett moved closer to examine her brother. Her husband followed close behind. "He looks somewhat pale," she said.

"I apologize, Mrs. Daggett. There were some, er, complications this afternoon due to your father's request that the viewing take place today. I will fix everything for tomorrow. I promise."

Kim nodded and began to look at the flower arrangements. She leaned toward her husband and whispered, "I have a feeling it's going to be a long night."

"Are you all right? Do you want me to give the okay to let the people outside in? It may be a little early, but it is snowing out there."

She checked one of the envelopes she brought with her in the box. Inside each was a coin for the people to get home safely, a piece of sugar-free candy, and piece of red thread. The candy was meant to remind people that there is sweetness in life as well as grief. Visitors were expected to consume the candy before they left the wake, destroy the envelope which represents sadness, and fasten the red string to their door to protect against evil spirits. It was a tradition she didn't believe in, but which she followed as a sign of respect and honor to her parents.

"Let me just check some of the flowers." She walked slowly around the room. Huge stands of lilies, chrysanthemums, carnations, and roses lined the walls. They came from friends of her father and mother, owners of beauty salons, laundry shops, and restaurants. There were baskets from Chinese American banks, the Chinese American Culture Association, the Metropolitan Life Insurance Company, the Snug Harbor Cultural Center, the Lieutenants' Benevolent Association, and the College of Staten Island. She paused at her brother's body lying in his casket. His right hand covered his left and the pinkie finger he broke playing basketball. The makeup on his face and hands was thick. Too thick, she thought. No one was going to say, "He looks like he's just sleeping." No, there was no mistaking it. Jimmy looked dead.

Kim turned and nodded to her husband to let the people outside in. Then she stood looking down at her brother and whispered, "The old must die, Jimmy, but, unfortunately, the young can die, too."

* * * *

Cavanaugh parked across the street from the Grub Funeral Home. He cradled the bouquet of red carnations under one arm as he walked through the snow flakes. Looking at the funeral home, he thought it resembled a haunted house from one of the Saturday morning cartoons. He half-expected to see Scooby-Doo and his mystery gang greet him at the door. Instead, Coppolino greeted him with, "Well, look who's here! If it isn't the famous Detective Cavanaugh himself! How the hell are you? I didn't believe it when they told me you retired. I figured you'd be one of those guys who died with his boots on."

"People change."

Coppolino leaned over and grabbed his arm. Cavanaugh pulled back.

"Easy, cowboy...."

Cavanaugh immediately remembered the woman in the Fed Ex parking lot. Those were her exact words. He got a bad feeling again. Was this some kind of an omen?

"I just wanted to give you some advice."

"You must have changed, Coppolino. The guy I used to know wouldn't give ice away on an iceberg."

"Very funny. I see you haven't lost your sarcastic sense of humor. I just wanted to give you a heads up and warn you about the red flowers you have. You don't bring red flowers to a Chinese wake. They're bad luck or something." He turned to Marotta for confirmation.

Marotta agreed. "He's right, Cavanaugh, but I don't think it's bad luck. It's more like an etiquette thing. In the Chinese culture, red symbolizes happiness, and happiness isn't exactly appropriate at the death of a young person, particularly a murdered young person."

Cavanaugh examined the flowers he held. "Thanks, guys. I'd better take these back to my car. By the way, have either of you seen my old partner, Morty Goldberg, around here?"

Both men said they didn't know him, and Cavanaugh walked back to his car. On the way, he saw a large Moravian Florist truck pull around the parking lot and make a delivery to the back of the building. The bad feeling came back to him just as a hand tapped him on the shoulder. He jumped back like a cat on a hot stove almost dropping the bouquet into the snow.

It was Goldberg.

*   *   *   *

Sgt. Anthony was kicking at the closet door and cursing loudly when Fr. Bennis returned to Greta's house. "He's been like this since he regained consciousness. I was about to call the police. I can't stand the man."

Bennis opened the closet and looked down at Anthony. "You have one choice, Malchus. Behave yourself or we call the police and let them deal with you."

"You wouldn't do that! They'll arrest you, too."

"I'd be long gone by the time they get here. And face it, who's going to believe a homeless, alcoholic, murderer or a priest? I'm sure Greta will support my story."

As Anthony struggled to get on his feet, Greta backed up holding a long kitchen broom over her shoulder in a threatening way. Bennis stood on the ready. All three stood standing and looking at each other. An eerie silence was suddenly shattered by the sound of a rooster's crow. Bennis and Anthony turned to see the cuckoo clock on the wall announcing the hour.

"Okay. You win this one. Do you think the lady who hates me could get me something to eat? I'm real hungry."

Bennis turned to Greta. "We are going to have to work together on this. Malchus knows things that might help us get Gretchen. We need his cooperation. Can you bury your hostility to him for Gretchen's sake?"

"This isn't about a little thing. It's not like he stole a cookie from the cookie jar. He hurt someone I loved."

"You love Gretchen, too. I know it's hard to let go of hate. But hate can consume you. It can destroy you, and everything you love. There are a lot of things in life that anger us. If you let them, they can control your life. Let God deal with those things. He promised to be there for us. Mother Teresa said, 'People are often unreasonable, irrational, and self-centered. Forgive them anyway…. In the final analysis, it is between you and God. It was never between you and them anyway.' It's natural to be angry, Greta, but anger can be poisonous and deadly. You may not like Malchus, but don't let that anger destroy the things you love."

"That's easier said than done, Jack. You don't know what he did."

"No. But you don't know where he's coming from either. I've been where you are, Greta. I know firsthand how anger and hatred can destroy all the good things in life. You may never forget, but try to forgive. It won't happen overnight, but give it a chance. Love never fails. It always protects, always trusts, always hopes, and always perseveres. If all else fails, think of Gretchen and your love for her."

"You can't believe that, Jack."

"But I do. I've seen how hate destroys a person. I've been there. It deprives a person of happiness. Work with me on this one, Greta. You asked me to help and I'm trying my best. It's for Gretchen. Please."

Greta slowly lowered the broom. She looked at both men and said, "We can eat in the kitchen. I'll fix some soup and sandwiches."

Anthony held out his hands to be untied and said, "Would you happen to have a couple of cold beers while you're at it?"

"If I were you, I wouldn't push your luck, Malchus," Bennis said as he started to untie him.

* * * *

Fran Cavanaugh and her sister Susan were trying to comfort little Stephen when Rosemary Palladino and a tall red-headed doctor appeared at the door. Stephen turned and smiled. The doctor came in and patted Stephen on the head and started examining him.

Nurse Palladino introduced the doctor to Fran and Susan. "This is Dr. Coyle. He's our resident pediatric doctor."

Coyle continued to examine Stephen's hands, chest, and feet as he said, "It's a pleasure to meet you."

Susan frowned and shrugged.

Dr. Coyle listened to Stephen's chest and checked the swollen lymph glands in his neck. He never turned to look at either woman. Finally, Susan addressed the back of his head. "What exactly is this Kawasaki Syndrome?"

He straightened up and stared at both women and then at Nurse Palladino. "No one explained this to you?"

"Actually, Dr. G. explained it to me and my husband, but I honestly don't completely understand what it is and don't have a clue how to explain it to Susan."

Coyle wrapped his stethoscope around his neck and rubbed his chin. "Hmm, I see. We actually don't know the cause of Kawasaki. It's probably from an infection of some sort or an abnormal immunologic response to an infection. It is by far not a common disease. Dr. G. was spot on in correctly identifying it. Since it is rarely seen, it may have been diagnosed as the flu or prolonged cold. You are, indeed, fortunate Dr. G. correctly diagnosed it. It usually occurs in children less than five years of age and is characterized by prolonged fever, exanthema, conjunctivitis, mucous membrane inflammation, cervical lymphadenopathy, and polyarthritis of variable severity."

"Wow! Exanthema and lymphadenopathy? Who would have thought? I haven't heard those words since medical school."

"Excuse me. I didn't know you were a doctor."

"She's not, Doctor. My sister is being facetious."

"You know, Doctor, like 'facetious' as in treating serious issues with deliberately inappropriate humor. All I'm asking for is for you to speak English. How the hell is a normal person going to know what exanthema and lymphadenopathy mean?"

Dr. Coyle's face turned the color of his hair. "I apologize. It's been a long day."

"It's been a long day for all of us. Maybe if you took the time to actually look at the person you are speaking to and not act like a pompous know-it-all automoton, patients and families would get a better understanding about what you are talking about and feel more relieved."

Dr. Coyle turned to Nurse Palladino who backed away.

Susan looked at him and said, "Doctor, you may be a terrific doctor, but you have the bedside manner of an ice cube."

He took a deep breath. "You are right. I apologize. Sometimes I get carried away. My wife tells me the same thing. I was rushing through my rounds. I should have been more considerate. Exanthema is a skin rash accompanied by a fever. Usually the fever in this case comes first and lasts for a week or two. Within five days, a red rash develops on the chest. Lymphyangitis is an infection of the lymph nodes. That's why I checked the lymph glands in the child's neck."

"Thank you, Doctor. That didn't hurt now, did it? I appreciate your translation of medical gobbledygook for the less educated. I don't know why so many medical professionals don't explain things in a way patients and families understand. It adds to a lot of needless fear and anxiety. Common courtesy and empathy are valuable skills too often lacking in some of the medical people I seem to have come across recently. By the way, the child's name is Stephen."

"I apologize. You were right. I'll try to learn from this experience."

"One more question, Doctor," Fran said. "What's Stephen's prognosis?"

Dr. Coyle rubbed his chin again and checked his chart. "The most important complications are those involving cardiac inflammation. That's why we took another EKG and echocardiogram. Arrhythmias, irregular heartbeats, can occur as the rash and fever begin to subside. That's why we want to be on top of it. On the positive side, he has been responding to the large dosages of aspirin. We are closely monitoring his progress. Believe me, Mrs. Cavanaugh, there is no need to worry at this time."

Fran and Susan thanked the doctor and, as he and Nurse Palladino left, Fran thought about his last comment about there being no need to worry *at this time*. Wasn't that, she thought, what General Custer said to his men as they rode into Little Bighorn?

* * * *

After giving Goldberg the black panties and asking him to have the DNA on them compared to the DNA of the murder victims, Cavanaugh joined the line into the funeral home. It was still snowing lightly. Although the severed bodies found in Martling's Pond and the Silver Lake Reservoir had neither heads nor hands, Cavanaugh thought blood, muscle, skin or even toe nails would contain DNA to be checked against possible vaginal stains or rubbed off skin cells on the black panties. Goldberg argued if Anthony used the underwear as a handkerchief the results of any testing might be compromised. When he finally convinced Goldberg to give it a try, they argued about the time needed for the testing. Cavanaugh emphasized the need for speed and pleaded on behalf of his brother to try to pull a few strings. If all else failed, he felt both Mayor Juliano and Police Commissioner Forster would expedite the testing if they thought it would lead to a speedy capture of the Staten Island Butcher. In return, Cavanaugh promised to turn Sgt. Anthony over to him.

Both Cavanaugh and Goldberg knew it was a long shot. But it was something. If the DNA matched one of the murder victims, for some reason, Father Bennis thought it would lead them to the killer. Cavanaugh needed more information. There was something his brother was holding out on him. After a quick condolence visit with Lt. Daggett, he planned to call his brother and find out why he wanted the DNA test results. If the DNA on the underwear matched one of the victims, his brother was giving the police enough evidence to arrest Sgt. Anthony for all the murders.

When he entered the funeral home, he shook some of the snow off and looked around. He spotted Steve Impellizzieri leaning against a wall in Jimmy Chen's visitation room. Impellizzieri wore a black suit, white shirt, and black tie. His bald head glistened under a recessed light in the ceiling. Cavanaugh approached him as Impellizzieri was scrutinizing the swaying derriere of a beautiful woman with long black hair walking by him.

"Stevie, you're getting to look more like Kojak every day. All you need now is a pair of shades and a lollipop."

Impellizzieri broke off his stare and looked at Cavanaugh in surprise. "I haven't seen you in a dog's age. How the hell have you been?"

"Fine. I've got a son now. I just dropped by to pay my respects. I used to work with Lt. Daggett."

"I got you beat. I've three curtain climbers and I'm

working on wife number three." He nodded toward the woman in a long, flared black trench coat and high leather boots who just passed by. "She's some knock-out. She could be a freaking beauty queen."

"If you like, I'll introduce you."

"You know her?"

"No, but I'll find out before I leave. First, you have to give me some info. I've never attended a Chinese wake before. Before I make any more mistakes, is there anything I need to know."

"You'll introduce me? Honest?"

"Honest."

"Okay. This wake is a little different. Usually, they last longer, but this one is only two nights. I don't know why, but I don't ask questions. First, no hand shaking. Just bow politely. The dead guy's sister will probably give you an envelope. In it will be a coin supposedly to get you home safely and a piece of candy. You're supposed to eat the candy before you leave and destroy the envelope. The envelope is bad luck. You leave it here. There may be some other things in the envelope, but I don't know what they're for. You don't have to worry about them."

Cavanaugh thanked him and moved behind the woman Impellizzieri had been ogling. He thought she smelled like lilacs, but that could have been from all the flowers around the room. The woman bowed at Kim Daggett and expressed her sympathies. He noticed Lt. Daggett standing by his wife. Matt Daggett recognized Cavanaugh and embraced him warmly. "I didn't expect to see you here, Cavanaugh," he exclaimed.

"I saw it in the paper and came to express my sorrow for your loss."

Daggett turned to his wife who was still talking to the woman with the long black hair. "Kim, let me introduce you to

Tom Cavanaugh. He's the guy I used to tell you stories about."

She turned and frowned. "Are you the guy who held the suspect off the roof of the precinct to get him to confess?"

Cavanaugh glanced at Matt Daggett and then at his wife and the woman with long black hair. "I'm not sure I recollect that incident, Mrs. Daggett."

"I believe they call that 'plausible deniability'," the woman next to him said.

"I'm sorry," Kim said, "this is Professor Deborah Edelman Russell. She was one of Jimmy's professors at the College of Staten Island."

Cavanaugh smiled and bowed. "It's a pleasure to meet you, Professor. To tell you the truth, I used to have a photographic memory, but it was never developed."

"You're very funny, Detective."

"That's not what a lot of people think, but thank you. What subject do you teach at the college?"

"I had Jimmy in my creative writing class. He was an excellent student. We all mourn his loss."

"It's a pleasure to meet you, Professor Russell."

"You can call me Deborah, Tom. But you must tell me more about these stories Matt tells about you."

Cavanaugh started to blush. "Deborah is a beautiful name, and it certainly fits a beautiful person like yourself. Did you know in the Old Testament, Deborah was known for her wisdom and strength? She was a poet, a judge, and a prophet and probably the only woman who gained fame by her own merit and not because of her relationship with a man."

"Thank you for those lovely comments, but I would really like to hear more about your experiences."

"I'm afraid, Deborah, those stories may be exaggerated somewhat and if I told you the truth I may have to kill you."

Professor Edelman Russell's eyes opened wide, and she took a step back.

"I'm only kidding," Cavanaugh said and pointed to Impellizzieri staring at him from the corner. "But if you really want to hear some good stories that man over there with the bald head could tell you some good ones. You can ask him about the elderly woman he tasered after she attacked a clerk with her shopping cart and started waving a gun at the workers because they wouldn't honor her coupon for one dollar or the deaf man he arrested for cursing at him in sign language."

She smiled, and he said, "I'll take you over and introduce you after I pay my respects."

* * * *

Otto Grub stood at the entrance to his office. "Did you see that woman in the black trench coat who just went by?"

Suadela answered softly, "Grub, you are insatiable. You already have someone."

"She's not cooperating. I'm going to have to get rid of her."

"Don't be foolish. Wait till the wake is over. There are too many people around now."

"I need to know the name of that woman? Who is she?"

"How do I know, asshole? Check out the funeral guest book if you are so excited. But be careful. The sister's husband is a cop, and there are cops all over the place. Use your head. Don't be stupid."

Grub adjusted his tie and twirled his moustache. He walked casually through the mourners and inspected the guest book. He didn't find her name. "Now what do I do, Suadela? She hasn't signed the book."

"Relax, Otto," she whispered in his ear. "You still have

Gretchen downstairs."

"But I want that woman. You don't understand how much I want her."

He walked into the visitation room and scrutinized the crowd. Then he saw her talking to Kim Daggett. His heart skipped a beat. "What's wrong?" Suadela asked.

"That man with them. I've seen him before." He locked eyes on the man and backed away. "He saw me at The Waterview Restaurant. He stared at me. What's he doing here?"

"It's probably just a coincidence."

"No. I pay attention to details. He was with that priest and the bum in the Army jacket. I saw him staring at me in the restaurant."

"Look at him. He's smiling and talking to the Daggetts and the woman. He hasn't recognized you. Relax. Even if he did, that doesn't mean anything. You are getting too nervous. Go back to your office and stay there until closing. I will keep watch on that man. Relax. You have nothing to worry about. He hasn't recognized you."

Grub felt a cold shiver sweep over his body. He walked back to his office, closed the door and sat behind his desk. His hands were shaking. Suadela was right. The man did not recognize him. He was safe. He was getting paranoid. She was right again. Even if he did, there was nothing to connect him to Gretchen. He closed his eyes and started fantasizing about how he would torture Gretchen before he killed her. The woman in the black trench coat would be his next victim.

But Otto Grub was wrong. Cavanaugh had recognized him.

* * * *

Cavanaugh saw Grub standing at the entrance to the visitation room scanning the mourners. He recognized him immediately. He remembered the eerie way he saw him staring at Gretchen Leone, the missing waitress. He had a bad feeling then, and he had a bad feeling now. Who was the man in the three-piece herringbone suit, the slicked back black hair and the Salvador Dali moustache?

Out of the corner of his eye, he saw the man back away suddenly. His detective's instincts kicked in again as he led the professor toward Impellizzieri who was grinning like the Cheshire Cat in Alice's *Adventures in Wonderland*. There were video surveillance cameras and a motion detection system all over the room. He wondered why a funeral home would need such an elaborate security system.

He noticed a gas fireplace along the side wall. It added warmth to the abnormally cool temperature in the room, but there was something strange about it. After introducing Santos and Impellizzieri, Cavanaugh stood in front of the fireplace and stared at the blue flames. Then he noticed it. There were ashes in the fireplace. What were ashes doing in a gas burning fireplace? He looked closer. It looked like remnants of clothing and possibly a running shoe were nestled behind the stack of large ceramic wood logs.

He watched the professor give her number to Impellizzieri and saunter away. "I owe you a solid, Cavanaugh. We have a date for coffee at the diner after the funeral."

"It must be the bald head. I hear some women find it attractive. I guess there's no accounting for taste. Make sure you shine that head of yours and try not to say too much. Once she gets to know you, she'll drop you like your other wives."

"Very funny. Actually, she said she'd like to write a story about my experiences as a cop."

"Now that is funny! Just do me two big favors: leave me out of your stories and tell me who the ghoulish guy I saw wandering around in the three-piece suit and the Salvador Dali moustache is."

"That's Otto Grub, the owner of the place. Do you want me to see if he needs more help? You could be a pallbearer. He pays pretty well and it's all off the books."

"No thanks. What can you tell me about him?"

"Not much really. He's kind of weird if you ask me. He's a loner. He had some of the guys design and put in a fancy security system for him. I don't know why he needed it, but he paid well. He's breaking Scamardella's balls tonight. He has him carrying the flowers from the parking area in the back upstairs. I don't know why, but he locked down the elevator. He's like a security nut if you ask me."

"What do the other guys think of him?"

"Pretty much the same thing. He's a fanatic on details. He gave each of us a specific job and told us to keep everything peaceful and not to go wandering around."

Cavanaugh shook Impellizzieri's hand. "If I were Italian, I'd hug you and give you a big juicy kiss, but where I come from this is all you get. If the professor asks you about what college you went to, what are you going to say?"

"Geez, I don't know. I barely got out of high school. What should I tell her?"

"You'll want to impress her. If I were you, I'd tell her you went to Georgia Tech and were on the football team. That should do it. If she asks what you majored in, tell her you majored in arithmetic. That should be good enough to really impress her."

*　*　*　*

Fran Cavanaugh was sitting in the semi-darkness of

her son's hospital room when Doctor Gianvito dropped by to check on Stephen. She was trying to think positive, but all her thoughts managed to turn negative. Dr. Coyle said there was no need to worry. But why did he have to add "at this time"? He said arrhythmias can occur. She took out her iPhone and googled "arrhythmias." She knew it was an irregular heartbeat, but how serious could that be? She had seen the television commercials for all sorts of drugs for treating atrial fibrillation or A-Fib. Her mother's brother, Uncle Carmine, had A-Fib, and he said he took rat poison for it. Actually, she knew he took warfarin which was originally developed by the Wisconsin Alumni Research Foundation as a means of killing rats.

But as she read up on A-Fib she discovered a lot of people had it including Ellen Degeneres, Howie Mandel, Elton John, and Jerry Jones, the owner of the Dallas Cowboys. That should have given Fran some solace, but her mind focused on people like such as Ted Williams, Mother Teresa, Arnold Palmer, Roger Moore and her own Uncle Carmine who were all dead.

She remembered how her husband always told her she had a tendency to look on the dark side. Instead of seeing the glass half filled with water, she saw it as half empty and wondered who drank the other half. Tom could call her a pessimist, but she knew blood clots could form in people with A-Fib, and if the clot broke free it could travel to the brain and cause a stroke.

Perhaps she was making too much of this. The doctor told her there was nothing to worry about. Why did she always catastrophize? Why couldn't she comfort herself with being ignorant? It was easier that way. If you didn't know what could possibly go wrong, you wouldn't worry about things that may not happen.

She leaned over and studied Stephen's face. He

looked so peaceful despite the monitoring tubes. He was so innocent, so young, so vulnerable. Why would God do this to him? Was God punishing her by making Stephen sick? She knew it was better to think about good things than to dwell on negative thoughts. But the more she tried, the more the negatives flashed across her brain. She remembered how Jack Bennis told her God allows us to suffer and to enjoy because He has given us the freedom to act as we will. He quoted Matthew 7:7, "Ask and it will be given to you; seek and you will find; knock and the door will be opened to you."

Fran folded her hands and began to pray. "Please, make Stephen better. I'm asking. No, I'm begging. Please, make him better. You promised that if I asked, it would be given. Please, I'm pleading. Make him better...."

Then she became aware of another presence in the room. She looked up with tearing eyes at Dr. Gianvito.

"I was just passing by, Fran, and I wanted to check on Stephen."

He looked tired. "How long have you been standing there?"

"Not that long. I didn't know if anyone told you about the latest test results. I thought you'd like to know."

Fran wiped her eyes. She didn't like the look on his face. He had bad news. She knew it. It must be so hard for doctors to give families the bad news. Do they ever get used to it?

"I can see you're worried, Fran. There's an old Swedish proverb my mother used to always tell us. 'Fear less, hope more; eat less, chew more; whine less, breathe more; talk less, say more; love more, and all good things will be yours.' It's actually pretty good advice."

She clasped her hands together and raised them to her chin. She glanced at Stephen and then up at Dr. Gianvito. "I'm ready, Doctor. Tell me the bad news."

He patted Stephen's head, checked the monitors, and looked at Fran. "I'm not sure I can do that."

She gasped and suppressed a cry.

"There is no bad news, Fran. Dr. Coyle told me you were worried so he and I stayed to check the lab results. Dr. Coyle is actually a very kind and competent doctor. The lab results were fine. There are no signs of cardiac inflammation or any arrhythmias. Stephen should be fine. It looks like your prayers were answered."

She rose and threw her arms around him. "Thank you, Dr. G."

"No need to thank me. Maybe it's that God of yours you should be thanking. As I recall, Stephen like me, was born with a veil or a caul. It's a membrane that covers a newborn's head. They call us "caulbearers" and we're considered to be extremely lucky and possess special talents. They say Charlemagne, Alexander the Great, Napoleon, Sigmund Freud and Albert Einstein were all born with a veil. Only 1 out of 80,000 births are born with a veil. It's even rarer than Kawasaki disease. Stephen and I are very special people, Fran. I wouldn't worry about him. He's going to be okay."

Fran's only thoughts were about what her own mother used to say. "From your lips to God's ears."

*   *   *   *

When Cavanaugh came out of Otto Grub's Funeral Home, a long line of mourners stood waiting at the entrance of the funeral home. Across the street Fred's Fish and Tackle Store was sandwiched between a pharmacy and a nail salon. Cavanaugh noted Fred's store looked directly into the funeral home's parking lot. Signs in the window of Fred's advertised scuba lessons, fishing trips, and live bait. If anyone could tell him more about Grub's Funeral Home, Cavanaugh figured someone in the store might.

The smell of fish and smoke hit Cavanaugh as soon as he entered the store. All around him hung displays of fishing rods and reels, nets, hooks, lures, gaffs and gigs, fish grippers, rulers, scales, crab nets, waders, fishing clothing and all kinds of accessories. To say the store was cluttered would be a gross understatement. Behind the counter was a diminutive man with a weathered face and deep set lines that could have been etched into his skin with a fillet knife. He wore a white embroidered cotton yacht captain's hat with the classic gold rope. His rolled up sleeves revealed an anchor and chain tattoo with the words "Liberty before Death" and "Death before Dishonor." He was reading a copy of *Sport Fishing* with a corncob pipe dangling from his mouth. When the man looked up, Cavanaugh saw he had a black patch over his left eye.

"Evening," the man said. "How can I help you?"

"Just looking, thank you. I just came from the wake across the street. I see you sell live bait."

"Yeah. I was fishing this morning when I ran out of worms. Then I saw this cottonmouth with a frog in its mouth. Frogs make pretty good bait, so I grabbed the snake. I knew it couldn't bit me with a frog in its mouth. I pulled the frog out of its mouth and threw the snake into my bucket."

"What did you do with the snake?"

"That was the problem. How could I get rid of the snake without getting bitten? Well, I'll tell you, I grabbed my bottle of Jack Daniels and poured a little into the snake's mouth. Its eyes got glassy and it went limp. Then I took it, threw it into the lake, and went back to fishing using the frog as bait."

"That was smart."

"It was, I agree, but a little while later, I felt something on my foot. It was the damn snake again. This time it brought me back two more frogs."

"Good story. I have to remember that one."

"You a cop?"

Cavanaugh straightened up. "Why would you say that?"

"You look and sound like one, and I wouldn't be surprised. That Grub guy across the street is a weird son of a bitch."

"Actually, I was on the job, but I'm retired. But what's with the guy?"

"He's a loner. Makes all the arrangements himself. Doesn't talk to anyone. Works alone unless he has business like now. There's just something about him that's darn-right creepy. "

"I don't particularly like funeral homes myself."

"That's not it. I've been in this place for almost forty years. I was here when his father was alive, and I don't think we've ever said more than two words to each other. As a kid he used to chase my sister and all the girls on the block with dead rats. He even left one on our doorstep. I imagine his kindergarten teacher gave him a U in 'works well with others.' He's like a lone wolf. Just the other night, I saw him unload something heavy from his car himself."

"You mean he picked up the body himself?"

"I don't know what he picked up, but it wasn't the Chen kid. No. He picked up the Chen kid this morning. This was the night before. I couldn't sleep. Sometimes my eye bothers me." He pointed to his patch. "I looked out and it was raining like a cow pissing on a flat rock. But there he was pulling a gurney out of his garage and loading something onto the gurney. What kind of guy does something like that in the wee hours of the morning in a downpour without help?"

"What was it he was unloading? Was it a body?"

"I don't know for sure, but it sure as hell could have been."

Cavanaugh remembered the two glasses of white wine Grub ordered at The Waterview. "Is he married or does he have any close friends?"

"Can't say. Might be. They say most of us crawl into the grave married. But I never saw anybody with him. Like I said, he's a loner. Sometimes I see him walking around talking to himself. Marriage will sometimes do that to a fellow. I'm telling you, mister, the guy is weird."

"Does he drink a lot? I think I would if I worked with dead bodies all my life."

"No. I don't think so. He's always dressed in a dark three-piece suit. I think he might even sleep in his suit. I'm telling you, the guy is just officially weird."

Cavanaugh smiled and thanked him. As he was turning to leave, he asked, "Sorry about your eye. How did it happen? Fishing accident?"

The captain laughed. "No. I don't know why I'm telling you this. Maybe it's because you're obviously not a fisherman, but I use it for effect." He pointed to his tattoo. "I was never in the Navy either. They are part of the mystique. I sell more fishing equipment because of the patch and the tattoo. People think I'm a character and come to hear me tell them stories of my adventures on the high seas. Just between the two of us, I've never been on a ship larger than a fishing boat." He paused for a moment to adjust his patch. "I guess that makes me kind of weird, too, doesn't it?"

"I think we are all weird in our own way," Cavanaugh said with a grin. "I know it runs in my family."

* * * *

Greta Johnson brought two bowls of chicken noodle soup, two ham and cheese sandwiches, and some bread to her kitchen table. Malchus Anthony rolled up the sleeves of his cassock. "I wouldn't want your precious dress to get dirty now, would I, Jack?" Bennis noticed two tattoos on Anthony's forearms. On his right arm was a spear and on his left what appeared like a cartoon character holding an oval shape beneath its legs. "Interesting tattoos, Malchus," he commented.

Greta put down her tea and stared at the figures on his arms. "Gretchen had some tattoos too, but I don't know what they meant. I doubt she even does. I honestly don't know why people bother marking up their bodies with drawings. As you age they fade and lose their shape. It's a barbaric custom if you ask me. "

Anthony picked up his sandwich and mumbled, "Nobody asked you."

Father Bennis studied the images on Anthony's arms and then said to Greta, "Most tattoos have meaning. These, I think, were carefully chosen."

Anthony smiled as he ate in silence.

"The one on the right, I believe, is an image of the Spear of Destiny. There are a lot of stories about that one. Some believe it is the Holy Lance that pierced the side of Jesus on the cross. Supposedly, Constantine the Great embedded a nail used in the crucifixion into the lance and it has mystical powers. Some even say Adolf Hitler actually started World War II to get the Spear of Destiny and when he lost it he committed suicide."

Greta frowned. "You can't believe that nonsense, can you?"

Anthony laughed and held out his left arm for Greta to see better. "Father Know-It-All, why don't you tell her what this one means?"

"I can see what it is myself," Greta said. "Although why a grown man would choose to draw on his arm a cartoon figure holding a ring between its legs is beyond me."

Anthony started laughing so much he almost choked. "That ain't no ring between its legs!"

"It's a depiction of an ancient gargoyle, Greta. They are found all over Europe, but particularly in Ireland. You see them on a lot of churches. It's called a *sheela na gig*. It's said to protect against death and evil spirits."

"What's the ring between its legs supposed to mean?"

Bennis rubbed the scar on his forehead.

"If you ain't going to tell her, Jack, I sure as hell will." Anthony pointed to the oval shaped object between the cartoon-like figure. "Take a good look. That's my little Sheela and she's holding her vulva in her hands and pulling it real wide!"

Greta reached over and slapped his arm. "You are a God-damn lecherous, vulgar pig, Malchus Anthony! Why weren't you killed in Vietnam?"

"Ouch!" Anthony pulled his arm away. "What's the matter with you? Come on. I'm trying to be nice. I could have called it another name."

Greta turned to Bennis. "Jack, I don't know why you are associating with this slime ball. Were you lying to me when you said this thing on his arm was found in churches? Why would anyone adorn a church with this kind of thing?"

Bennis' cell phone started ringing. He looked at his phone and saw it was from his brother. Before answering it, he said, "There're a lot of theories about that, Greta. One theory is that the *sheela na gigs* were intended to warn against lust, covetousness, and sins of the flesh."

Anthony laughed out loud again. "If that's the case, Jack, it sure as hell didn't work with me now, did it?"

* * * *

VIII

When Cavanaugh arrived at the address his brother gave him, an inch of wet snow covered the lawn and clung to the trees. He rang the doorbell and waited. No one came. Maybe this was the wrong house. He looked around. There were no other footprints but his in the snow. Could the snow have covered other footprints? Was this another of his brother's tests to see if he were followed? He shivered as he watched the snow fall around him. He could see a light on inside the house. He rang the doorbell again. No one answered.

He was cold and frustrated. He felt his temper rising. Was his brother playing games with him again? He pounded his fist on the wooden door.

Then he heard the chain on the door being released, and the door slowly opened. An older woman in a housecoat stood there looking at him. She wore no makeup. The lines on her face were deep. Her hair was streaked with gray. But her deep set eyes were bright and alert. She said nothing as she held the door with one hand.

"I'm sorry if I have disturbed you. I'm looking for my brother. He told me I could reach him at this address."

The woman narrowed the opening in the door and examined him from head to toe. Finally, she asked, "Who are you?"

"My name is Tom Cavanaugh."

"What's this brother of yours name supposed to be?"

"He's a priest. His name is Father Bennis."

"What makes you think this brother of yours would be in my house?"

"I'm sorry, lady, if I have disturbed you. It's snowing out and I'm cold and tired. I told you my brother said he would be here. If he's not, then I'm gone."

The woman opened the door wider and looked down the street. "Is that your car across the street?"

"Yes."

"Pull it into the driveway and come in when you are ready."

"Is my brother here?"

"I don't usually invite strangers into my house. Yes. He is here. Now hurry up and move your car."

Cavanaugh did as instructed. When he entered the house, he found the woman, his brother, and Sgt. Anthony sitting at the kitchen table. "What's Anthony doing here?" he shouted at his brother.

Father Bennis rose and held up his hands. "Relax, Thomas. We have a lot to tell you. Malchus is helping us."

"Helping you? Are you kidding me? The cops are looking for both of you for beating up a teenager in a bodega in Mariners Harbor. I just passed the place on the way to the wake, and the police are still there."

"That's a misunderstanding, Thomas. Malchus was defending the storekeeper."

"Defending the storekeeper? He almost killed that kid!"

The woman grabbed Father Bennis' arm. "I told you he was bad, Jack. We need to turn him over to the police."

Sgt. Anthony stood and gripped his spoon in an aggressive position. "Nobody's taking me to the police without a fight."

Bennis shook his head. "Will everyone please calm down and take a seat? We have a lot to explain and not much time if we are going to locate Gretchen."

After a long moment of indecision, one by one they sat around the table. Fr. Bennis described how Anthony found the black panties he used as a handkerchief in the garbage by the bodega where they went for a sandwich.

"We never got that sandwich either!" Anthony interrupted.

"Stifle it, Malchus."

"Hold on, Jack. He said he found the panties in the bodega's garbage?"

"Yes. But that's not all. He found other women's clothes in the garbage, too. That's why I gave the panties to you to give to Goldberg to check for DNA. I think they may belong to one of the killer's victims."

"That's a long shot, Jack. It could be anyone throwing clothes away."

"Based on his description of the bras found in the garbage the clothes belonged to at least two different people."

The woman spoke. "Malchus Anthony, you are a disgusting, loathsome pig!"

Cavanaugh frowned. He looked at his brother with raised eyebrows.

"I'm sorry, Thomas. I didn't introduce you. This is Greta Johnson. She is Gretchen's grandmother."

"Hold on. You think whoever dumped the clothes is the killer?"

"It's conceivable. And it's the only real clue we have. I don't think the killer would be stupid enough to put the clothes in his own garbage, but I think whoever he is, he lives somewhere in that area."

Cavanaugh bit his lip. "Is there anything else you have to add?"

"Tell him about the black car I saw," Anthony said.

"I almost forgot. Malchus saw a big, black car stop and pick someone up on the road alongside of the Chinese Scholar's Garden the night of Gretchen's disappearance. The car stopped, picked someone up, and then fishtailed up the street. If Gretchen were walking, that would be the most logical street she would have taken."

Cavanaugh stretched and scratched his head. "I admit I thought you were crazy when you told me Anthony wasn't the Staten Island Butcher, but now I have to agree with you. I do think he killed the kid in the Chinese Garden, but the other murders don't fit."

"Where do we go from here? I thought Malchus may be able to identify the car, but we drove around the neighborhood and didn't see anything that resembled the black car or van he saw."

"I think I may have stumbled on the killer tonight," Cavanaugh said. Greta Johnson, Malchus Anthony, and Jack Bennis stared at him. "I went to Jimmy Chen's wake tonight. It's just up the block from that bodega. It turns out the funeral director is Otto Grub. He happens to be the creepy guy we saw in The Waterview Restaurant eyeballing Gretchen. Funeral homes use big, black cars. I nosed around a bit and found this Grub character is a bit weird. He has an elaborate security system that includes motion detection devices. In the back of a gas burning fireplace, I saw what looked like ashes from clothes and part of a running shoe."

"We have got to get in there."

"That's easier said than done. We have no real proof. The police would never be able to get a search warrant on the theories we have."

"You have to get in there and save our granddaughter!" Greta said.

Cavanaugh looked at his brother who was rubbing the scar above his eye. No one spoke for a long while.

* * * *

"The Lord is my shepherd; I shall not want. He maketh me to lie down in green pastures: he leadeth me beside the still waters." Considering where she was, Gretchen knew this wasn't the most appropriate prayer as she huddled beneath the soft white taffeta and lace lining on the cold concrete floor of the Grub Funeral Home, but it was the first one that came to her memory.

" Yea, though I walk through the valley of the shadow of death, I will fear no evil: for thou art with me; thy rod and thy staff they comfort me." But she was afraid. She looked at the bobbing heads of Grub's previous victims looking down at her. She had seen the bones of Sophia Bellini being ground up into a fine dust. Was this the fate that God had intended for her? Her grandmother made her read Elisabeth Kübler-Ross' book *On Death and Dying* when her mother died. Back then, she had gone through the stages of denial and isolation, anger, bargaining, depression, and finally acceptance. It took time, but with her grandmother's help she came to accept what had happened. But this was different. No one was coming to rescue her. He was going to kill her. The question was, what would he do to her before he killed her?

"Surely goodness and mercy shall follow me all the days of my life: and I will dwell in the house of the Lord forever." But goodness and mercy hadn't followed her. Maybe if she had gone to church more often, things would be different. She doubted that as the sad eyes above her seemed to shake their heads. It hadn't worked for them. Why should it work for her? Her grandmother had taught her there are some things in life we cannot change. This seemed to be one of them. But it was so difficult to accept.

She dreaded to think what the future would bring. She dreaded his look, his voice, his smell, his touch, the pain. She closed her eyes and tried to think of something else, anything else. And then she heard the voice of Mr. Bennis reading Joyce Kilmer's poem in her English class, "I think that I shall never see / A poem lovely as a tree...." She could see him standing in front of the class. "A tree that looks at God all day, / And lifts her leafy arms to pray...."

She made one more desperate effort to free herself, but it was useless. She knew it. She shook her head and wished she had been a better person. And then she prayed. It was all she had left. As Mr. Bennis' words echoed in her mind, she began to see the reason he said, "There are no atheists in foxholes."

* * * *

Otto Grub told Scamardella, Marotta, Impellizzieri, and Coppolino to usher everyone out of his funeral home by 10:00 p.m. He wanted to get back to Gretchen. At Suadela's urging, he would give her one more chance to cooperate with his desires. If she resisted he would beat her and torture her like he had done to the others. He embraced Suadela's suggestion to dismember her piece by piece. He would start with her toes and then her fingers. The more he thought about it, the more aroused he became.

A series of loud knocks on his office door broke his reverie. It was Impellizzieri. Everyone had gone, except for four people who refused to go. They insisted it was their right and duty to show honor to the deceased by staying the entire night.

Grub told Impellizzieri to get Marotta, Scamardella, and Coppolino and meet him in the viewing room. When he had left, he turned to Suadela and asked, "Now what am I going to do? I can't have them staying the whole night. I need to get back to Gretchen."

"You are pathetic, Grub. This is your business. Tell them only members of the immediate family are permitted to stay. Chen's sister left with her husband. Have your cop friends escort them off the premises."

"But what if they insist?"

"Tell them if they don't leave, they will be arrested for trespassing or unlawful assembly."

Grub stood, straightened his tie, and walked to the viewing room. His hands were shaking. There in the back of the room was one overweight Asian man with three friends. They had brought cards, chips, and food with them. The overweight man looked like he could have been a Sumo wrestler. He stood as Grub approached. "We are going to stay the night to protect the spirit of Jimmy Chen," he said.

Grub's voice trembled as he asked, "Are you immediate family members?"

"We're here to pay our respect."

"I apologize, gentlemen, but the Designation of the Intentions which was signed by the deceased's sister strictly prohibits anyone but immediate family from staying the entire night."

The big man put his hands on his hips and frowned. "I don't understand. Where is she? I need to talk to her."

"Unfortunately, she left, and I am afraid you gentlemen will have to leave, too."

The three other men stood and stared at Grub. The tallest and skinniest man reached into his jacket pocket. Impellizzieri, Marotta, Scamardella and Coppolino spread out and surrounded the men as they moved their hands toward their weapons.

"Gentlemen, it is the law. We are not looking for any trouble. If you do not leave immediately, I will have to have these men arrest you for trespassing. The decision is yours."

Impellizzieri, Marotta, Scamardella, and Coppolino gave each other furtive looks, but said nothing.

The big man made a grunting sound and then headed for the door followed by his friends. He said something in Mandarin and the others chuckled. When everyone had left, Grub turned, locked the doors, and turned on his security system. He was tired, but looking forward to playing with his "prize" in the basemen.

Unlocking the elevator, Grub felt Suadela slide in beside him. "Enjoy yourself, Otto. To see others suffer does one good, to make others suffer is even better. Without cruelty there can be no enjoyment! When you have corrupted this Gretchen bitch, made her abandon her moral center, and brought out a writhing, mewling, bucking, wonton whore for your enjoyment and pleasure, then, believe me, she will be more beautiful than ever. Enjoy yourself, Otto, and I will enjoy her with you!"

* * * *

Father Bennis closed his eyes and rubbed the scar on his forehead. "I remember him now."

"Who?"

"Otto Grub, the funeral director. I said a Requiem Mass

at Our Lady Help of Christians for a 98 year old man who was buried from his place. I should have remembered him."

"So what are we going to do?"

"We have to get in there and check if Gretchen is there."

Sgt. Anthony shoved a piece of white bread into his mouth and said what everyone was thinking. "What's the fucking rush? He's probably killed her already."

Greta Johnson threw her empty cup and saucer at Anthony. "You selfish animal! I hate you!" she sobbed as he ducked and the cup crashed into the wall.

Fr. Bennis put his arm around Greta's shoulder. "It's not over yet. If he has her, we will find her."

"And how the hell are you going to do that?" Anthony asked. "Your brother already told you the place is secured like Ft. Knox with surveillance cameras and motion detectors. You can't even get into the place. If the cops see you, they'll lock you up. You can't get a search warrant. It's useless."

Cavanaugh put his hands on the table. "It's not over until the fat lady sings."

"And what the hell is that supposed to mean?"

"I've got an idea. We create a diversion."

Jack Bennis looked at his brother. "What are you thinking, Thomas?"

"I've been reading this book about the OSS during World War II while watching Stephen in the hospital. There was this guy, Dr. Stanley Lovell, who was in charge of developing creative psychological weapons to use in the war. Lovell was motivation for the character Q in the James Bond movies. He created a lot of bizarre 'out-of-the-box' gadgets and operations to confuse, demoralize, and infiltrate the enemy. Some of the things they came up with were amazing. They made truth drugs, booby-trap explosives disguised as cow shit, guns disguised as pens and cigarette packs, compasses disguised as uniform buttons, and a plastic explosive they called 'Aunt Jermina' that looked like baking flour."

"What's your point, Thomas?"

"I can create a diversion which will clear the funeral home out. Anthony brings some flowers to the back and distracts the ex-cop back there while you, Jack, sneak in and check out the place. Once you find some proof that Gretchen is there, send me a text and I'll have Goldberg and the cops raid the place."

"Do you think it will work?"

"If we all do our job, it will work like a charm."

"Why do I have to get involved?" Anthony asked. "It sounds like a harebrained scheme to me."

"Nobody's asking you."

"Trust me, Anthony. I know the guy accepting the flowers. Scamardella is easily distracted. All you have to do is distract him."

"And how the hell am I supposed to do that?"

"After you give him the flowers, pretend to faint. He'll try to help you and then Jack can slip in behind him and check out the place. It should be a piece of cake."

Greta folded her arms. "I wouldn't trust him if my life depended on it let alone my granddaughter's life. Let me go instead of him."

"The basket of flowers is too heavy," Cavanaugh said. "Scamardella wouldn't believe you were the delivery man."

"That sounds like a sexist remark!"

"It is what it is, Mrs. Johnson. Besides we're going to need you to call for reinforcements if anything goes wrong."

"I thought you said this plan would work like a charm. Like what could go wrong?"

"Scamardella might catch Jack. We'll need you to explain what he was doing there and why. They're not going to accept my explanation. They'll think I'm just making excuses for my brother."

"So what am I supposed to do?" she asked. "Stand here waiting for the phone to ring?"

Bennis wiped a tear rolling down Greta's cheek. "You sound just like your granddaughter. When I was teaching Milton's poem 'On His Blindness,' she had a hard time understanding his final lines, 'They also serve who only stand and wait.'"

Anthony coughed and leaned forward. "If she's so hell bent on doing something, she can take my place."

"No way, Malchus," Bennis said. "You and I are going together. You owe it to me."

"I don't need you or nobody else. And I don't owe you shit!"

Cavanaugh reached across the table and grasped Anthony's arm. "Listen, Anthony, I have no problem calling the police right now and turning you in. The only reason I haven't done so already is my brother. He wants to find Mrs. Johnson's granddaughter and we're going to help him. Make up your mind right now. You're either in this with us or I'm going to make sure they lock your sorry ass up for murdering Jimmy Chen."

Anthony raised his hands in mock-surrender. "All right. All right. I'll go along with this, but you have to promise to tell the cops how I helped you."

Cavanaugh and Bennis agreed. Greta, however, shook her head. "I still don't trust him."

"He's all we've got right now, Greta. If we're going to get Gretchen, we need him."

"I just don't trust him, Jack. He's a selfish sack of shit."

Malchus Anthony leaned forward and hissed, "The feelings mutual, bitch."

* * * *

IX

An uneasy truce had settled on the Johnson house when Cavanaugh's wife called from the hospital to tell him the good news about Stephen's test results. In light of the good news, Fran suggested that Cavanaugh come home as Stephen was being well taken care of in the hospital, and they both needed the rest. Cavanaugh agreed. There were some things he would need to prepare for their assault on the Grub Funeral Home the following night.

Before he left, they went over the plans again for breaking into the funeral home. Bennis and Anthony would stay at Greta Johnson's house and await Cavanaugh's call the next day. He went out to his car and brought in the large basket of red carnations. He gave Anthony specific instructions about the time to make his delivery and how to distract Scamardella. Once Scamardella was distracted, Father Bennis would sneak into the home and begin to search for any clues to Gretchen's disappearance. When he found something, he would call Cavanaugh and Johnson. They all believed it was a long shot, but it was all they had.

Given Otto Grub's strange behaviors, Anthony's finding women's clothing not far from his funeral home, the large black car Anthony saw picking someone up on the route Gretchen would have taken home, and the remnants of clothing Cavanaugh saw in the gas fireplace, Cavanaugh and Bennis believed Grub could be holding Gretchen somewhere in his funeral home. Right now it was circumstantial evidence and not enough to warrant a search warrant. If Goldberg were able to determine DNA on the black underwear Anthony had matched one of the murder victims it would place the sergeant as the chief suspect in the killings, but it would supply them with an added degree of certainty that Otto Grub was the "Staten Island Butcher."

Pulling out of the Johnson driveway, Cavanaugh knew how he planned to create a panic in the funeral home. Timing was critical. Once his brother had entered the funeral home, he would create a disturbance that would hopefully cause an evacuation of the premises. He knew his plan had not worked perfectly for the French Resistance during World War II, but given the particular circumstances of Jimmy Chen's wake, he felt confident it would work here. He had seen it clear out a PBA meeting with delegates in Brooklyn.

At the corner of the block, he saw a car in his rear view mirror start up and start to follow him. He made a left at the next corner, and the car followed. He made a right at the next corner, and the car was still behind him. He accelerated and made a quick right a few blocks ahead and pulled over to the curb. He shut his lights off and waited. Then he checked his side view mirror and saw a dark blue Volkswagen Jetta quickly make the turn.

Cavanaugh pulled out and followed the Jetta. Why was someone following him? At the next block he pulled alongside of the car and cut it off. He jumped out of his car and approached the Jetta. A young woman sat behind the wheel of the car. She looked frightened. He pounded on her window as the snow fell around him. "Why were you following me, lady?" he demanded.

She slowly lowered her window. "You are Detective Cavanaugh, aren't you?"

"It's 'former' Detective Cavanaugh. I retired. And who the hell are you and why are you following me?"

"I saw you at Jimmy Chen's wake. I recognized you."

"I'm going to ask you one more time, lady. Who are you?"

She fumbled in her purse and Cavanaugh drew his pistol. "I wouldn't advise you to try anything. I can't miss at this range."

"No. Please. I'm a reporter. My name is Lucy Bauer. I work for CBS News."

"And why are you following me?"

I thought I could ask you some questions about Jimmy Chen, but when you drove to Greta Johnson's house I became curious. I tried to interview her, but she slammed the door in my face."

"It's called respecting someone's privacy."

"But how do you know her? And why did she let you in?"

Cavanaugh smiled and shook some of the snow off him. "I have to hand it to you. You're curious, persistent, and good-looking, too, but I'm tired and on my way home. Good night, Ms. Bauer."

"No. Wait. Please. I need a story. Tell me something I can give my editor."

"Jimmy Chen's murder and Greta Johnson are totally unrelated. I just dropped by to pay my condolences. End of story."

"At this late hour, Mr. Cavanaugh?"

Cavanaugh turned, shook his head, and said, "I'm going home now. You must know where I live. There's no need to follow me. Good night, Ms. Bauer."

* * * *

Fran was sitting on the sofa listening to the late news on 1010 WINS when Cavanaugh returned home. She looked up at him as he came into the room. "You look tired, Tom. Where were you? The wake must have been over hours ago."

"It was, Fran. I dropped by to see my brother."

"Is he all right?"

Cavanaugh walked to the kitchen and pulled a bottle of Becks from the refrigerator. Fran followed him. "What's going on, Tom?"

"It's a long story. Jack's got himself involved again. This time he's trying to find his former student whom we met at the restaurant the other day. She's gone missing."

"Yes. I heard that on the news. They think she might have been taken by the same person who dropped those bodies into Marling's Pond and the Silver Lake Reservoir. They still haven't found Sophia Bellini yet either. I heard her parents on the radio again appealing for information on their daughter. There's even a reward offered for information. The fear is she too will end up all cut up and floating in the water one of these days."

Cavanaugh took a long slug of beer, plopped down at the kitchen table, and shook his head. "So how is Stephen doing?"

"The doctors expedited the test results, and they say things look good. I don't know what I'd do if anything happened to him."

Cavanaugh gulped another mouthful of beer.

"I hope he doesn't develop a heart condition over this. I've been reading on the Internet how there are a lot of possible cardiac problems developing from Kawasaki disease. What if Stephen develops a heart condition?"

Cavanaugh finished his beer and reached into the refrigerator for another one.

"You're not listening to me, Tom! I'm talking about our son!"

Cavanaugh popped the cap on the beer bottle and stared at Fran. "You're catastrophizing again. What did the doctors say? They said the test results were good. Why is it that not good is never enough for you? Why do you have to explore every possible disaster known to mankind? Am I concerned about him? Of course, I am. He's my son, too. But you have to let the doctors do what they have to do."

"But what if he develops aneurysms or ectasia?"

"For God's sake, Fran, you've been reading too much on the Internet! Do you even know what ectasia is?"

"Not exactly, but it is a possible effect of Kawasaki disease."

Cavanaugh banged his beer bottle on the table and foam started bubbling out. "I've read that shit on the Internet, too. And I also read with early treatment of the disease, a fast recovery is expected and the risk of coronary problems is greatly reduced."

"But what if ...?"

"Then we deal with it. Right now he's getting better. That's a good thing."

"I don't know how you can be so cavalier about this whole thing."

"*Cavalier*?" Cavanaugh took two more gulps of beer and appeared to calm down. "Maybe I am, Fran, but not in the way you think. I love Stephen and would give my life for him. He's in good hands. I'm not going to worry about what could possibly go wrong. If it does, we'll deal with it. Right now, it's my brother I'm more worried about. He's gotten himself into some trouble."

"What kind of trouble?"

"It's complicated, Fran. Let's just say he's harboring a killer whom the police think is the Staten Island Butcher, and the police are looking for him."

Fran got up and pulled a bottle of white wine from the refrigerator and poured a glass for herself. "I don't understand. Jack is a priest. Why would he involve himself with a murderer?"

"Like I said, it's complicated. Jack doesn't think this guy is the Staten Island Butcher, and he's been looking for clues to the disappearance of Gretchen Leone, his former student and our waitress from the other day. If you take some of the clues he has uncovered with some of the facts I uncovered tonight at the wake, I think he might be right."

"Tell me you are not getting involved in this, too!"

"We don't have enough solid proof yet to go to the police."

"No, Tom! You're not doing this again. The last time you tried to help your brother we almost all got killed. Don't get me wrong. I love your brother, but it's like trouble follows him like a dark shadow."

Cavanaugh began to scrape the label off his beer bottle. "I can't leave him out there by himself, Fran. He's my brother. He needs my help."

"Tell him to go to the police."

"You don't understand. He can't. They'll arrest the man he is protecting and him for being an accessory. And the real Staten Island Butcher will still be out there."

"I don't like this."

"We have a plan. If it works, we will find the real killer and hopefully rescue Gretchen Leone if she is still alive."

"What kind of a plan?"

"Don't worry. We've got everything taken care of."

"I seem to remember you saying the same thing before. I *really* don't like this!"

"And I don't like guacamole, avocado, tripe, buttermilk, tofu, and self-serving politicians. We can avoid some of the things we don't like, but we have to deal with some of them, too. Now let's get to bed. We're both tired, and tomorrow promises to be an interesting day."

* * * *

When the concealed door slid open, Otto Grub stepped into his "playroom." First, he checked the severed heads floating in the jars on the shelf and nodded. They were beautiful. He paused in front of each one and grinned. He remembered each one and the joy he experienced in "playing" with them. "They were good times, Suadela. I can still recall the feel of their skin, their smells, and their screams." Then he turned and looked at Gretchen. She was cowering in the corner beneath the white taffeta and lace casket lining he had given her.

"Well now, sweetheart, are you ready to cooperate?"

Gretchen looked up at him. "Please," she sobbed, "no more. Please, I'm begging you. Let me go."

Otto laughed. "Did you hear that, Suadela? She's begging me to let her go." He reached down and yanked the lining off her. "There, that's more like it. Let's see your beautiful body."

Gretchen scrunched up and clasped her knees to her chest.

"Now, now, Gretchen, there's no need to be like that. We can have some fun together. I really don't want to hurt you." Slowly he began to undress. He took off his jacket and folded it neatly on one of the tables. Then he unbuttoned his vest, and then removed his tie and shirt.

Gretchen closed her eyes. She was shivering.

Grub removed his trousers and underwear, but kept his shoes and socks on. "Look at me, Gretchen. I am here for you." He leaned down and grasped her leg. She resisted and stiffened. "You're not cooperating, Gretchen!" he shouted. He yanked her leg and pulled her away from the pole her arm was attached to.

She screamed.

"Relax, Gretchen. Enjoy yourself. Some of the others made the most of their moments with me. Alas, poor Sophia fought me and you saw what happened to her."

She kicked at him with her other foot hitting him in the groin. "What difference does it make? You're going to kill me anyway like you did with all the others."

Grub turned and looked at Suadela. "She doesn't get it, Suadela."

Gretchen started to say something in a soft whisper. He released her leg and bent to listen. She was praying, "The Lord is my Shepard; I shall not want...."

"You need to teach her a lesson, Otto," Suadela said. "Show her what a difference pain makes."

And then Otto Grub grinned and began to kick Gretchen with his shoes and beat her with his belt. He continued until his arms and legs grew tired, and Gretchen lay bleeding and motionless on the concrete floor.

*   *   *   *

Greta Johnson gave Father Bennis and Sergeant Anthony the guestroom to sleep in. The room was neat and clean, but the wallpaper and furniture made it look like they had stepped into a time warp machine and were back in the 1960s. The wallpaper displayed aqua and purple flowers separated by a blue checkered strip on a white textured background. There were two nightstands, a twin sized bed, a six drawer dresser, a desk and a chair, and a vanity with a large mirror. All the furniture was French Provincial ivory with gold trim. On the desk, stood a Motorola Ranger transistor radio and a white Murano glass lamp with a circular pattern on a brass base. A duplicate lamp was on the night table by the bed along with a Westclox travel alarm clock. On the wall opposite the bed, a GE portable television with two antennae rested in a white cabinet. The only pictures on the wall were a photo of John F. Kennedy and a faded print of van Gogh's "Starry Night."

The two men stood at the door speechless. Finally, Sgt. Anthony said, "If you think I'm sleeping in that bed with you, you're fucking nuts."

"The feeling is mutual. You take the bed. I'll sleep on the floor."

Anthony didn't argue. He plopped down on the bed immediately. Bennis sat on the desk chair. Anthony threw him a throw pillow case cover with aqua and purple flowers matching the wallpaper. "Here, take this. And let me give you a little advice. I wouldn't trust that woman out there with your jock strap. She's a God damn liar."

"What are you talking about?"

"I never raped nobody."

"But you said...."

"I was bull shitting and so was she."

"I don't understand. Why would the both of you say that? How did she know you?"

"It's a long story, Jack. And frankly I'm too tired. Just remember what I told you. Don't trust her."

Jack Bennis looked at Anthony as he turned over in the bed and was asleep in less than a minute. Why had Anthony said that? Was he telling the truth? Was Greta telling the truth? Was Gretchen really his granddaughter? Could this have all been a ploy to get him involved with finding Gretchen? Why did she hate Anthony so much? How did they know each other?

He looked at the mirror over the vanity and saw he was rubbing the scar on his forehead. If she were lying, how did she know about the scar and about his covert missions? Somewhere in the back of his brain, he recalled Pascal's Wager about the existence of God. If God does not exist, one could lead an immoral life with no consequences. But if God does exist and one leads an immoral life there will be consequences. Therefore, Pascal thought, it is better to lead a moral life whether God exists or not. Would Bennis act differently if Gretchen were not his granddaughter? But what if she were, and he did nothing? What was the truth, and in the end did it really matter?

Bennis got up and walked around the room. Thoughts kept jumping around in his head like fleas on a dog. What was it the Countess said in Shakespeare's *All's Well That Ends Well*? "Love all, trust a few, do wrong to none." That was good advice that he frequently failed to follow. Did he trust Malchus Anthony? No, not really.

Anthony's snoring drowned out his moving the six drawer dresser to block possible egress through the window. Then he bedded down by the door. If Anthony tried to escape he would have either to move the dresser or to move him. He didn't trust Anthony, but he was part of the plan to find Gretchen whether she really was his granddaughter or not and whether she was alive or already dead.

* * * *

X

Cavanaugh didn't sleep well that night. He ran through scenario after scenario about what could possibly go wrong with their plan.

Number 1: Sgt. Anthony was a "loose cannon." He didn't trust him.

Number 2: His brother followed his own drummer. Could he be depended upon to stick to the plan and get out of the funeral home as soon as he found evidence?

Number 3: The tension between Greta Johnson and Malchus Anthony could be another problem.

Number 4: There was that nosey CBS reporter, Lucy Bauer. What if she followed him? She could mess up the whole plan.

Number 5: Of course, a lot depended on Goldberg and the DNA match. What if he couldn't match the DNA on the black panties to one of the murder victims? If they were caught, it would be a case of breaking and entering to add to the already accumulating charges against his brother. Then again, what if the DNA did match? Would that be all the evidence the police needed to arrest Anthony as the Staten Island Butcher? What if his brother was right and Anthony was not the real killer?

There were more holes in his plan than in a sponge or a honeycomb.

He didn't tell the others how he planned to create a disturbance at the wake. If they knew, they would think he was crazy. And maybe he was – at least a little bit. But then again, weren't we all to some degree or another?

At 2:00 a.m., he crept out of bed, turned on his computer and went online. Cavanaugh had long been interested in things most people would describe as trivia. He wanted to verify what he was reading in the book in the hospital about America's Office of Strategic Services (OSS) during World War II. He read how the OSS conducted multiple missions involving spying and sabotage and how General "Wild Bill" Donovan encouraged his Research and Development team to "think outside the box" in developing unique tools in the fight against Nazi Germany and Imperialist Japan. His Director of Research and Development was Dr. Stanley Lovell. The more Cavanaugh read about Lovell, the more he admired him. Lovell's mission was to develop "miscellaneous weapons" to fight the enemy. He was tasked with throwing all previous law-abiding concepts of war out the window and using whatever resources were available. Lovell's devious, creative imagination, indeed, earned him the nickname "Professor Moriority."

Some of Dr. Lovell's wily devices worked, and some did not. He once attempted to capture bats above the Pennsylvania Hotel in order to use the bats as incendiary bomb carriers. He oversaw the development of "caccolube" which when added to the oil of an engine would destroy it in thirty minutes. He developed "Hedy," a panic creator that simulated the sound of falling bombs and explosions. He designed silencers and flash suppressors for guns, uniform buttons which were actually compasses, exploding candles, miniature cameras, a device to blow the wheels of trains, and a single-shot weapon the size of a golfer's pencil.

But the diabolical gadget that most intrigued Cavanaugh was Lovell's secret weapon called "Who Me?"

Cavanaugh had used something like this at a PBA meeting on topic "New York City's Marijuana Laws and the Stop and Frisk Procedures," and it worked like a charm. Within minutes the entire room cleared. Some people were angry, but Cavanaugh didn't care. He wasn't the least bit interested in laws and regulations the Mayor at that time proposed. If he saw someone buying or selling marijuana or possibly in possession of a firearm, he would bust him or her.

What he had done at the PBA meeting was basically what he planned to do at Grub's Funeral Home. Dr. Lovell's policy was to use anything that might aid the war, whether unorthodox, untried, or even comical. "Who Me?" was a top secret highly concentrated stink spray that smelled like fecal matter. It was originally intended to spray on enemy officers to humiliate them, but it was difficult to control and often the sprayer smelled worse than the sprayed. What Cavanaugh used at the PBA meeting were stink bombs he obtained at a novelty store. They were in glass vials that he casually dropped or threw around the room. When they broke or were stepped on, a noxious smell permeated the entire room.

Cavanaugh considered himself a good detective. Part of his skill was his ability to compartmentalize. His focus was intense. If he were working a case, that was all that mattered. He didn't worry about other people's feelings.

He learned at Jimmy Chen's wake that ritual was important in Chinese families. He confirmed this in his Google searches. If poor Jimmy started to stink, it would create a panic. Cavanaugh knew it wasn't a "nice" thing to do at a wake, and it would upset the family of the deceased, but he had done worse things as a cop. He recalled some of his "unorthodox" methods of interrogating criminal suspects to get confessions. He wasn't particularly proud of what he did, but he did get the confessions and the arrests. He remembered how Matt Daggett had worked with him on some of these unusual "enhanced interrogation" methods when they were patrolmen in Brooklyn.

He knew if his brother knew what he was planning he would call it sacrilegious. Jack Bennis would argue Cavanaugh's plan was disrespectful, irreverent, and blasphemous. And that was the reason he didn't tell him or anyone else how he planned to create the diversion needed for Jack to sneak into the funeral home. In the morning, Cavanaugh planned to go to the novelty store in the Mall and pick up some stink bombs and fart spray. If Gretchen Leone was alive or dead and if everything went as planned, they would have the evidence needed to arrest Otto Grub. That was – if everything went as planned.

* * * *

Detective Goldberg hand delivered the black panties and asked that the tests be expedited. He had long been fascinated by the use of DNA in crime situations. DNA, or Deoxyribonucleic Acid, had been studied for many years as the generic building block in all things. But it wasn't until over twenty years ago that a professor at the University of Leicester proved the uniqueness of DNA in each person's skin, blood, body fluids, nails and hair. DNA proved to be more reliable than shoe prints, blood, clothing, and even eye witnesses and partial fingerprints. It could be used to identify individuals based on only partial remains. In 2012, New York

State recognized DNA as a major aid in solving crimes and required any defendant convicted of a misdemeanor or felony give a DNA sample to be added to the New York State DNA Databank.

DNA was a major game changer in solving crimes. Blood found at a crime scene deteriorates with time, but DNA results remain viable for an indefinite period of time. Indeed, a number of rape and murder convictions were overturned by recent analyses of DNA results which had not previously been available. Thus far, there had been no DNA matches from the partial remains found in Martling's Pond and the Clove Lake Reservoir. If DNA taken from the black panties Cavanaugh gave him matched the DNA of one of the victims, it could be the break in the case they were looking for.

Goldberg gave the panties to Jimmy Monreale, a thin, serious lab technician, whom he had grown to trust. After explaining the need for haste, he asked, "Can you get me the results by tomorrow at the latest?"

"Are you serious, Detective? Look at all the files I have on my desk. I have a backload of tests to do. Everyone wants everything yesterday."

"This is really important. We are trying to stop a serial killer. I know if I were asking for a paternity test I could get it in a day. You have got to be able to rush this test."

"With all due respect, Detective, you have no idea what you are asking for. This is not McDonalds or Burger King. The turnaround time for DNA testing in some states ranges from twenty days to up to two years. Look around. Do you see anyone here helping me? No. Of course not, I'm just a lab technician. All the bosses have gone home hours ago."

"Come on, Jimmy. We are trying to save lives here. This is New York. I read about a company that developed a machine that can analyze DNA samples in less than two hours. I think forensics labs are using it in Florida now."

Lab technician Monreale stood up, adjusted his glasses, and shook his head. "Yes, Detective, this *is* New York where we have become accustomed to long wait times, traffic delays, high costs, limited resources, bureaucratic waste, and political incompetency. The bottom line is I can't help you, Detective. Your request is above my pay grade."

Goldberg understood Monreale's situation, but he believed where there was a will, there was a way. He wasn't going to let this request die without a fight. He spoke with his Commanding Officer, Thomas Monahan, and emphasized the need for alacrity. Two young girls were missing. Two others were dead. He promised if the DNA on the panties matched the DNA from any of the girls, his source would surrender Sgt. Malchus Anthony. Goldberg pushed the envelope by suggesting the Police Commissioner and the Mayor might be able to expedite the DNA testing. "Based on the escalation of the kidnappings, the FBI thinks there will be more killings. If the press gets a hold of information that the police failed to act on credible leads, there will be hell to pay."

Monahan was a seasoned police officer with over thirty-five years on the force. He had seen mayors and police commissioners come and go. He had witnessed corruption and incompetence and everything in between. He thanked Goldberg for his initiative and promised to pursue the matter up to the governor if necessary.

That was last night. At noon, the following day, Morty Goldberg had not heard anything from anyone. He sat quietly at his temporary desk at the 120 Precinct staring at the phone. In his mind, he played back the Israeli National Anthem, *Hatikvah*, and prayed that hope was not lost and that they would soon stop the brutal killings and apprehend the Staten Island Butcher.

Then the phone rang.

*   *   *   *

"Detective Morton Goldberg, please."

"Yes. This is Detective Goldberg. How may I help you?"

"This is Greta Johnson. Have you located my granddaughter yet?"

"No, Mrs. Johnson, but we are pursuing some promising leads."

"What kind of leads?"

"I'm really not at liberty to say at this moment. As soon as I have additional information, I will contact you."

"That's what you told me before, but I haven't heard from you."

"I'm sorry, Mrs. Johnson, but investigations take time. Believe me we are doing all that we can to locate your granddaughter."

"Do you think that homeless Army sergeant, Malchus Anthony, had anything to do with my granddaughter's disappearance?"

Goldberg picked up a pencil. "Why would you say that?"

"You're not telling me everything, Detective Goldberg. There was an article in the *New York Post* this morning about this sergeant being a 'person of interest' in the murders and kidnappings."

"I personally don't know where the *Post* gets its 'alleged' information, Mrs. Johnson. I do know, however, you can't believe everything you read in the papers."

He paused and added, "If we have any additional information, rest assured I will forward it to you. I have your number. Have a good day, Mrs. Johnson." Then he hung up.

Goldberg didn't hear the phone being ripped from Greta Johnson's hand and a graveled voice saying, "What the hell do you think you're doing, woman?"

* * * *

Otto Grub's hands were shaking as he stepped into his shower. Suadela was right beside him. He turned on the hot water and cold water cascaded over him. He shivered and moved back. He looked down and watched clots of dried blood flowing down the drain. "It won't go away," he stammered. He grabbed the soap and began rubbing his arms and legs furiously. "Why is there so much blood?"

"Get hold of yourself, Otto. It's not your blood."

"But I can smell it. It won't go away."

"What a poor specimen of a human being you are! You want it all, but you are not willing to pay for the consequences."

As the hot water started to mingle with the cold, he reached to adjust the faucets. Red stained water circulated around his feet. He turned to Suadela. "Why is there so much blood? Is she dead?"

"If she's not, she will be shortly. You beat her very badly. How did it feel?"

He leaned his head back under the shower head and closed his eyes.

Suadela's voice was hard and sharp. "I told you that seeing others suffer is good, and how making them suffer is even better. You made Gretchen suffer for our mutual enjoyment and pleasure. Acknowledge it. You enjoyed every minute of it!"

He looked down at the clots of blood on the drain. "But the blood! There is so much of it!"

"It will wash away, and you will get another one. That woman you saw tonight in the long black trench coat and the high leather boots, she will do fine."

"But I don't know her name, Suadela. She never signed the guest book."

"Must I do everything for you? Sometimes I don't think you have the brains you were born with. You saw her talking to the Daggetts and then to that bald headed ex-cop. Ask them who she is."

"But I really liked Gretchen. I wish she had cooperated."

"She didn't. You did what you could, and she got what she deserved. Now it is time to find your next victim. I think the woman you saw last night will work out fine."

Grub folded his arms and stared through the streaming water at Suadela. "But... but you said that about the others, too."

Suadela's voice seemed to reverberate against the walls of the shower. "You insolent, little prig! How dare you question me! You ingrate! Have I not brought you nothing but happiness and pleasure? Where would your sorry ass be without me?"

Soap ran into his eyes. He closed his eyes and tried to wash the stinging away. When he opened his eyes, Suadela had left.

"I'm sorry, Suadela. I'm sorry!" he cried. "Please come back! Please come back!"

*   *   *   *

Father Bennis was making grilled cheese sandwiches in the kitchen when he heard the disturbance in the hall. He rushed out to see Greta Johnson beating Sgt. Anthony's chest with her fists. Anthony held the telephone high in his hand.

"What the hell is going on?"

"She called the police! The bitch was going to turn me in."

"I was not! I only wanted to find out more information."

Bennis pulled her away. "Greta, you can't do this! You can ruin this whole plan before it even gets off the ground."

"I just wanted to know if there was any new information on Gretchen."

Bennis held her arms against the wall and stared into her eyes. "*We* are the new information, Greta. If our plan works, I will find Gretchen and have her home to you tonight."

Sgt. Anthony waved the phone at her. "That's if you mind your own fucking business, and she ain't already dead!"

"Enough! Both of you take a break. We are not going to get anywhere if this keeps up." The priest directed each of them to a seat at the dining room table. "Now let me go over this one more time. Tom hasn't called yet so we don't know if the DNA on the underwear matches one of the victims. That means all we have as far as the police are concerned is circumstantial evidence. Basically, it's our 'theory' versus hard, cold facts. I believe we are on the right track, but we need proof. That's why I'm going into the funeral home tonight to look around. Malchus, your job is to distract the man assigned to collect the flowers. Tom will create a disturbance to create confusion. I will sneak in and look for Gretchen. When I find her, I will call you, Greta, and you will notify the police. Are we all clear on this? We are only going to have one chance on this. If we fail, the police will not be able to obtain a search warrant, and we may never be able to find Gretchen. From what we have pieced together thus far, I am pretty sure that this Otto Grub is the man who has been kidnapping these girls."

Greta Johnson lowered her head and said nothing.

Malchus Anthony stared at Greta. "I don't trust her, Jack. If she screws up, we're all screwed."

Greta's face was red. She gripped the edge of the table

with white knuckles. Slowly, she lifted her head. "I understand. I'll cooperate. It's my granddaughter we're talking about. She's all I have. I'll do what you want if it will bring her back to me."

Anthony wiped his nose with his hand. "If she's okay with this, I'm in. I don't know how she got you involved in this, Jack, but I'll go along with it. When this is all over, you better put a good word in for me with the cops." He softened his tone and turned to Greta. "Your granddaughter is lucky to have someone who will fight for her the way you do. It says somewhere in that book of Jack's that a good tree cannot bear bad fruit and a bad tree cannot bear good fruit. I guess I'm what you would call a bad tree. Maybe I can finally do something good. If all I have to do is distract the flower guy, I'm good for it."

Anthony extended his hand toward Greta. She looked at the hand as if it were contaminated with the widespread ulcerations and lesions of a leper.

Jack Bennis shattered a long moment of silence. "Greta, whatever happened in the past is over. We are talking about possibly saving your granddaughter's life. You asked me to help, and I'm trying to, but you have to help, too."

Reluctantly, she extended her hand, and she and Anthony shook hands just as the telephone rang. She pulled away like she had touched hot stove and reached for the phone.

It was Tom Cavanaugh. The DNA results had not come back yet. The plan was on. They synchronized their watches and reviewed their roles once more.

* * * *

Greta Johnson gave Sgt. Anthony some clothes left by Gretchen's father. They were tight, but he could get away with it. Beneath a worn Navy parker, he chose to wear a Hawaiian sports shirt with pineapples and palm trees.

The snow had stopped, but a fine, cold mist turned some of the freshly fallen snow on the ground into slush. Bennis drove to the parking lot of Grub's Funeral Home. He and Anthony got out of the car and went around to the trunk. They went over the plan again.

As Bennis reached into the car's trunk to pick up the basket of red carnations, Anthony sprang forward and gripped Bennis over his right shoulder and hooked the bend of his arm around Bennis' neck. Anthony's arms were like steel. He applied pressure with his biceps and forearms on both sides of Bennis' neck in a blood choke hold. The priest struggled. He tried to kick Anthony in the groin and stomp on his foot, but Anthony pulled back and down. Bennis tried to reach back at Anthony's eyes to gouge them, but the pressure from Anthony's arms on his carotid arteries cut off his air supply and the blood to his brain.

"This is for the sucker punch you gave me at Greta's," he whispered in Bennis' ear. "In a few seconds you'll be unconscious. Don't make me kill you. Just remember what I told you about her. Don't trust her."

When Bennis' body went limp, Anthony lifted him into the car's trunk. Then he walked around to the back of the funeral home where he saw Scamardella sitting on some boxes smoking a cigarette. He checked his watch. It was time.

Scamardella turned when he saw Anthony. "These are for the Chen funeral," Anthony said. "Where do you want me to bring them?"

"I'll take them from here." Looking at the red carnations, he said, "Shit, doesn't anyone know you don't send red flowers to a Chinese wake? They're bad luck." He never saw the hard right and then left to his temples as Anthony blindsided him. He dropped the carnations and crumbled into the slush. Quickly, Anthony bent down and rifled through Scamardella's wallet. He took all the cash and removed a chronograph stainless steel Timex watch from his wrist. Then, as an alarm sounded upstairs, he headed for the chain linked fence in the back leaving a trail of slushy footprints behind.

* * * *

Upstairs there was panic. The foul smell of human feces permeated the viewing room. "It's coming from Jimmy," someone shouted. People held their breath. "It's disgusting! I can't breathe! I need air!"

Otto Grub stood in his three piece black suit at the entrance to the room. He looked paler than usual.

"What's happening?" Kim Daggett asked. "Where's that smell coming from?"

"It's from Jimmy," a college student said gagging as he rushed past Grub and Daggett.

"This is disgusting! My father trusted you, Mr. Grub. What did you do to Jimmy?"

Mourners rushed past Grub choking and coughing. Some held handkerchiefs over their noses.

Grub stood paralyzed. "Do something, asshole," Suadela said.

An alarm sounded. "Everyone out!" Grub shouted. Marotta, Coppolino, and Impellizzieri ushered people out into the night air. "This is bad luck," an overweight Asian man commented as he waddled toward the exit.

Grub walked through the rancid smell. He traced the origin of the feces smell to Jimmy Chen's casket. On the carpet all around the room, he saw broken vials of glass.

"This is a deliberate act of sabotage," Suadela whispered in his ear. "You need to get everyone out."

Grub turned to Marotta. "Get Scamardella up here to help with getting everyone out."

Impellizzieri held his black jacket over his nose and mouth. "Have you notified the fire department?"

"No need," Grub answered. "Look around. Someone dropped stink bombs all over the room and sprayed some kind of fart spay on the casket."

"I think we should still notify the fire department."

"Absolutely not! Get everyone out! I'll deal with this myself." Grub looked up to see Marotta guiding Scamardella toward him. Scamardella was holding the side of his head.

"Somebody mugged Paulie," Marotta said.

"They got my watch and wallet. I had a couple of hundred bucks in my wallet."

"Sounds like this was well-planned. We need to call the police."

Grub's hands were shaking. "No! No need to call the police. It was probably just a college prank."

"College prank? My ass! The guy that slugged me was no college kid!"

Grub held up his hands. "No, please, no police. I will reimburse you for your losses. Just make sure everyone is out, and then I will lock everything up."

Marotta, Coppolino, Impellizzieri, and Scamardella looked at each other. "I really think we need to notify the police," Coppolino said. The others nodded agreement.

"No! It is settled. I will handle this myself. For your cooperation tonight, I will double your pay. It is important to me that we contain this situation. I do not want tonight's events publicized. It would be bad for business."

"You'll double our pay plus reimburse me for my losses?"

"Yes. I will double your pay if you all agree. But you need to let me handle this myself. Do I have your cooperation on this matter?"

The four men looked at each other and nodded. Grub walked them to the main entrance, locked the door, and then went back to his office and set his alarm system.

* * * *

Cavanaugh walked around the funeral home and waited in the semi-dark parking lot for the call from his brother. The crowd outside dispersed slowly. He still had the smell of fart spray on him. He looked at his watch. Gradually, one car after another drove out of the parking lot. It began to get colder. He checked his watch again. Why hadn't he heard from his brother? Fr. Bennis' car was at the end of the parking lot. The only other car in the lot was a 1978 Pontiac Trans Am. He looked around. Where was Malchus Anthony? He should have been in the car.

Then out of the shadows he saw a man walking toward the Trans Am. As the man got closer, he recognized him. It was Steve Impellizzieri. "Hey, Stevie, is this your heap?"

"Cavanaugh? Is that you? What the hell are you doing here?"

"Where did you get this bomb?"

"Eat your heart out! It's a classic."

"Man, Stevie, you smell like shit! Did you have an accident?"

"Very funny, Cavanaugh. Some guy dropped stink bombs in the viewing room. It caused a near panic. The funeral director was pissed."

"I saw everyone leaving. I think some of that smell might have gotten on me, too."

Impellizzieri fumbled for his car keys. "It's freaking cold out here. What are you still doing here?"

"I'm waiting for my brother. You didn't happen to see

him, did you? He's a priest."

"No. Things got pretty crazy in there. Some guy mugged Scamardella and stole his wallet and watch."

Cavanaugh frowned. "I didn't see any police. How come?"

"Grub, the funeral director, didn't want to call the cops. He said he would handle it himself. I think he's afraid of bad press."

Cavanaugh blew on his hands. "I don't blame him. Did Scamardella get a good look at the guy that mugged him?"

"No. He said he blindsided him. I thought it might have been a kid, but he claimed it was an old guy delivering flowers. Probably a drug addict."

"Sorry to hear that. Is he okay?"

"Yeah. Paulie's got a head like a rock. Actually, things worked out okay. Grub offered to double our pay and reimburse Paulie for his losses if we kept the police out of it."

Cavanaugh looked down at the only other car in the parking lot. He had a bad feeling again. "That's my brother's car down there. I think I'll go down there and wait for him. Take care and stay safe, Stevie."

"Thanks, Cavanaugh. And thanks for the intro to the Professor. She's one hot number."

"Go easy with her. Just remember what I told you about majoring in arithmetic in college. Believe me that will impress her. A lot of guys will be interested in her. "

Impellizzieri opened his car door. "Don't I know it! Even the funeral director was interested in her. He asked me a lot of questions about her. I think he might be interested in her, too."

Cavanaugh said good night and walked slowly toward his brother's car. The closer he got to it, the more his bad feeling grew.

The Staten Island Butcher

*   *   *   *

As Cavanaugh approached his brother's car, he saw a set of footprints leading around the building. This didn't make sense. There should have been two sets of footprints. Had Anthony overreacted? Had he attacked Scamardella when their initial plan didn't work? Cavanaugh stopped. There should have been two sets of footprints. One for Anthony and one for Bennis. His brother was supposed to enter the building after Anthony distracted Scamardella. He looked at the footprints in the slush and then at the car.

Then he heard it. It sounded like a dull hammering. Where was it coming from?

Then he heard a muffled voice. It was coming from the rear of his brother's car.

Cavanaugh ran to the car. The pounding was coming from the trunk. "Help! Help!" came from the trunk. "Get me out of here!"

"Is that you, Jack?"

"Yes! Get me out of here!"

Cavanaugh stood in the cold. He scratched his head. "How did you get in there?"

"Now is not the time for questions, Thomas. Just get me out of here."

Cavanaugh smiled. He placed his hand on the truck's lid. "How long have you been in there?"

Bennis kicked hard and one of the brake lights broke. "Come on, Thomas. Get me out of here!"

"You know you've dented the car with all your kicking."

"Open the trunk, Thomas! This is not funny. Anthony jumped me and shoved me in here."

Cavanaugh walked to the driver's door. "That old alcoholic bum got the jump on my invincible big brother? I don't believe it!"

185

"Where are you going? Get me out of here. Gretchen's life is in danger."

Cavanaugh reached in and released the trunk lock. Father Bennis was climbing out of the trunk when he turned around.

"Where did he go?"

Cavanaugh traced the footprint trail around the building. "Looks like your good friend went back to his old habits. I think he jumped Scamardella and stole his wallet and watch. I told you that you shouldn't trust him."

Bennis followed the footprints around the back of the building. At the delivery door, the snow was matted down and an overturned bouquet of red carnations lay in a puddle of slush against the building. "Looks like your good buddy mugged Paulie here and then took off in the direction of the fence in the back," Cavanaugh said.

Jack Bennis bent down and examined the slushy footprints. "Careful, you don't step in them," he said as he tracked the footprints to the chain linked fence. He stopped at the fence and used his cell phone to shine into the darkness beyond the fence.

"What are you doing, Jack?"

Bennis pointed into the dense evergreen foliage on the other side of the fence.

"What do you see, Thomas?"

"I think it's some kind of Arborvitae. People use them for privacy. Why? Is this another of your Jeopardy questions?"

"Look closely. What do you notice?"

"It's a pretty healthy shrub."

"If Anthony climbed over the fence here, you would expect the branches to be bent or broken. They're not."

Cavanaugh saw his brother was right.

Bennis shone his light on the trees. High up on one Scamardella's watch and wallet were nestled in the branches. "Anthony never climbed this fence. He threw the wallet and watch over."

"But why would he do that?"

Bennis squatted next to the footprints. "Look carefully, Thomas. The footprints lead to the fence, but if you observe the footprints more carefully, you can see a double imprint in the slush. After he mugged Scamardella he deliberately walked to the fence and then doubled back stepping carefully in his own footsteps."

Cavanaugh inspected the footprints. "You're right. He must have walked backwards, stepping into his previous footprints. But why?"

"He wanted us and everyone else to think he robbed Scamardella and then took off with his watch and money."

Cavanaugh looked at his brother. "Then where did he go?"

Bennis stared at the rear of the Grub Funeral Home. "I think he went in there instead of me."

"But why? This doesn't make sense."

Bennis rubbed the scar on his forehead. "I gave up trying to figure out why people do the things they do a long time ago. The question is, what do we do now?"

* * * *

Malchus Anthony hid behind unopened coffin crates. He heard some kind of commotion upstairs. Then a tall, muscular man with a bald head opened a door on the left and yelled. "Come on, Paulie, wake up! Grub wants all hands on deck upstairs to help control the mob. Somebody dropped stink bombs all over the place. It smells like shit up there."

Anthony peered out between the boxes to see the man crouch down next to the unconscious Paulie. "What the fuck happened? Are you okay?"

Paulie made some grunting noises and then, "Somebody slugged me." He struggled to his feet. "Some old guy was delivering flowers and he cold-cocked me."

The bald man helped Paulie to his feet. "What did he do?"

"He hit me! I just told you."

"Where did he go?"

"How the hell should I know? I was out cold!"

The bald man looked out into the night. He saw the footprints in the slush and snow leading away. "Looks like he took off. Did he get anything?"

Paulie patted his pockets. "Shit! The bastard took my wallet!" He felt his wrist. "And he took my watch!"

"Did he get your service revolver?"

Paulie reached down and felt his ankle. "No. He missed it."

"Good. Your wallet and watch can be replaced. He was probably a drug addict. It would be a real pain in the ass if he got your gun."

Malchus Anthony watched as the two men locked the door and headed for the stairs. Paulie was holding his head. The bald man's arm was around him. "Take it easy, big guy. We'll get the guy who did this?"

As they shut the lights off and started up the stairs, Anthony whispered to himself, "Not if I can help it."

*   *   *   *

XI

Father Bennis and Cavanaugh stood in the cold staring at the dark building in front of them. "Looks like your plan didn't work," Cavanaugh finally said.

"My plan? This was your plan from the beginning."

"If you didn't let Anthony get the jump on you, it would have worked. Face it, Jack. You're not the same guy you used to be."

Bennis turned to his brother. "I don't believe you. Whose idea was it to use fart spray to create a diversion?"

"How did you know?"

"Because you smell like shit! Who Me? Didn't work in World War II. What made you think it would work here?"

"How do you know about 'Who Me'?"

"You're not the only one who reads books, Thomas."

"Well, to be perfectly honest, it did work! It cleared the whole funeral home out. If you had done your part, you would be in there right now."

Bennis looked at the car trunk. "He surprised me. He's good. He grabbed me in a blood choke hold which cut off the blood supply to my brain. I was unconscious in less than ten seconds."

"Maybe he'll call us when he finds something."

"In case you didn't notice, he doesn't have a phone. Homeless people don't usually have a need for one."

"Never thought of that. Why do you think he did it? I thought he didn't want any part of this."

"I wish I knew. He said he didn't want to kill me and then something about Greta. He said I shouldn't trust her."

"Why would he say that?"

"I don't know, but there obviously is something going on between them. They don't trust each other."

Cavanaugh wrapped his arms around his chest. "It's freaking cold out here, Jack. What do you say we get some coffee and figure out what our next plan is?"

"I have to get in there, Thomas. I promised Greta I would find her granddaughter."

"Hold on, big brother. This whole thing doesn't make sense. Why are you so *gung-ho* about finding this former student of yours? I can understand your trying to help, but you've been risking your life. What's the story? There are things you are not telling me."

"It's complicated."

"Life's complicated. What's the story?"

The two men leaned against the car in the darkness. A light snow began to fall again. Jack Bennis slowly told the story to his brother. He told him about that night in Georgia, about drinking with Sgt. Anthony, about waking up in a motel room with no memory of how he got there. And he told him about Greta Johnson and how she knew so much about that night and how she recounted to him what happened.

"Do you think she was telling the truth?"

"I don't know, but she told me things I had never told anyone else."

"Do you really think Gretchen is your granddaughter?"

"I don't know. Greta told me she is. I can't take the chance that she's not."

"Anthony told you that you shouldn't trust her."

"They hate each other."

Cavanaugh stared at the dark building in front of them. "Then why would he choose to go in there by himself?"

* * * *

Malchus Anthony was familiar with the dark. He had crawled through damp tunnels in Vietnam and crawled through littered streets and alleys in cities across the country. He didn't need a gun. He felt something he hadn't felt in a long time. He was on a mission. Maybe the tree wasn't all bad, and some good fruit could still come out of it.

He recalled Cavanaugh saying there was an elaborate security system in the funeral home. He hadn't seen any cameras in the storage room he was in. Wherever there were cameras, there would need to be someone watching the cameras. Most likely, the video surveillance cameras and motion detection system were located upstairs in the viewing rooms. He waited in the dark, and his eyes became adjusted to the darkness.

He wasn't afraid of the dark here as he had been crawling through narrow, claustrophobic, intricate Viet Cong tunnels. Cameras didn't compare to rats and bugs, boobie traps, punji sticks laced with feces, and Bamboo Pit Viper snakes. He had inched his way through the tunnels by touch and smell like a blind man. He would never forget the telltale smell of sweat and strong spices on the Viet Cong. He knew they thought the Americans smelled of cigarettes and coffee.

As his eyes became adjusted to the darkness, he felt his way around the room. When he reached the door where

Paulie and the bald man had left, he smelled the faint odor of formaldehyde.

Carefully, he opened the door. Next to an elevator, a staircase led upstairs. He felt along the wall and proceeded down a long corridor. The smell of formaldehyde increased. At the end of the corridor, he ran into a wall. The smell was strongest here, but there was no door. He felt around the wall until his hand touched what felt like a button.

He hesitated. The button might be an alarm system. What did he have to lose? If he found the girl, he would have the proof that he was not the serial killer the police were after. His hand hovered over the button. If he pressed It, however, it might flood the room with light and he would be found without finding any proof about the girl's disappearance.

He thought about the girl. He had seen her in the restaurant and seen her picture in Greta Johnson's house. There was something about the girl - something familiar, something allusive. There was no doubt Greta hated him. He remembered her. He remembered the night they first met. She had cause to hate him, but he never did the things she said he did. Why had she lied?

Maybe she didn't lie – at least deliberately. Maybe because of her intense hatred of him she had transferred something that happened to someone else and assigned it to him. He had seen this happen in battle and on the streets. He recalled telling a group of homeless drunks in San Francisco about Jane Fonda trying to get him to drink with her to launch her husband Tom Hayden's campaign for the California State Assembly. He told them how he refused and called her a Commie and a traitor. Years later, he heard one of the men who had heard his story repeating it as if he had experienced it himself. He wasn't lying. He really believed he had met Fonda. He even used Anthony's exact expletives.

Because the memory was so vivid and strong to this person, he assumed that it came from his own experience. He had seen politicians and newscasters do the same thing.

Maybe if he found Gretchen, Greta would forgive him. Maybe he was getting soft. A lot of people hated him. It never bothered him before. Why did it now? He pictured Gretchen in his mind. There was something about the girl.

Death never bothered Anthony. He escaped it in Vietnam. He eluded it in the homeless shelters and streets and alleys around the world. He knew it was just a matter of time. He thought about his life. He had done a lot of bad things. Sometimes he wondered why he was still here. Sometimes he almost looked forward to death.

He recalled someone once saying to him, "No matter where you are, that's the place to be." He smiled. He was born on Staten Island, and here he was back on Staten Island. Maybe Grub's Funeral Home was the place he was meant to be.

He pushed the button.

Slowly, the wall slid open, and he was blinded by bright fluorescent lights. He choked at the overwhelming odor of formaldehyde and dampness. He closed his eyes and then squinted into the lighted room.

As his eyes became accustomed to the light, he looked around the room. In the far corner he saw a still body lying in a puddle of blood. It was a woman. A young woman. She was naked and badly beaten. One hand was handcuffed to an iron pole. On the wrist of the hand was a half-moon, half-sun tattoo like he had seen on the girl in the restaurant when she handed him the menu.

He had found Gretchen Leone. He felt for a pulse, but his hands shook and his heart beat so loudly, he didn't know if she had one. He looked around and saw a surgical table with an airbush hose, an autopsy saw, scissors, scalpels, clamps, and a variety of brushes and needles. Anthony grabbed a needle and a scalpel and went to work trying to open the handcuff.

His hands shook as he worked. He wished he had a drink. It would steady his nerves. He concentrated on opening the handcuffs. He worked with a passion he had not felt in a long time. He found Gretchen and the serial killer. Maybe the "bad tree" could finally bear some "good fruit" after all.

As he fumbled with the handcuffs, he felt the presence of something else in the room. He looked up and saw the floating heads looking down at him. But that wasn't it. He had seen severed heads before. There was something else in the room – something evil.

He reached down, grasped the scalpel, and turned.

* * * *

Outside a woman's voice called out from the darkness. "There you are. I've been looking all over for you."

Cavanaugh and Bennis turned. It was Lucy Bauer, the CBS reporter.

"It was you, wasn't it?"

Cavanaugh moved in front of his brother. "Ms. Bauer, I don't know what you're talking about."

"You set off that stink bomb in the funeral home."

"You have to be kidding. Why would I do something like that?"

She leaned in closer. "Who's the man in back of you?"

Cavanaugh held up his hands. "That's none of your business, Ms. Bauer. Please leave us alone before you get yourself into a lot of trouble."

"Are you threatening me, Mr. Cavanaugh?" She craned her neck to see the man behind Cavanaugh. "That's your brother, the priest, isn't it? The police are looking for him and that homeless dishonorably discharged soldier. Your brother has been harboring him. He killed the Chen boy."

"Please, Ms. Bauer, you don't understand."

As she pulled out her cell phone, Cavanaugh's phone rang. He looked at the number. It was his wife. He wanted to ignore it, but it might be about their son. "What is it, Fran? Is Stephen okay?"

"Yes. Everything is fine. The doctors say we can take him home tomorrow."

"Listen, Fran. I can't talk to you right now. I'm in the middle of something."

"Where are you? You sound anxious."

"Can't talk right now. I will call you back as soon as I can. Love you. Goodbye."

"Isn't that sweet! Now talk to me, Mr. Cavanaugh. What's the story?"

Bennis stepped around his brother. "You are right, Ms. Bauer. I am Father Jack Bennis, but you don't understand what is happening here."

"Jack, don't talk to her. She's a reporter. All she's interested in is a juicy story. The facts mean little to people like her."

"That's not true!" Bauer said. "I know Gretchen Leone was a former student of Father Bennis. I know she worked as a waitress at The Waterview Restaurant and that you two may have been among the last people to see her. I know former Sgt. Malchus Anthony was with you at the restaurant and his fingerprints were found at the scene of Jimmy Chen's murder."

"How do you know all that?"

"I have my sources. But there's more to the story. The police theorize that Anthony is the Staten Island Butcher, but that doesn't make sense to me. Where would a homeless alcoholic keep the missing women? Based on the dissected body parts recovered in the lakes, the police originally thought the killer must be a butcher, a doctor, or someone familiar with the human body. Anthony doesn't fit that profile."

"And who told you all of this?"

"I have my sources. I won't reveal their names. And if you choose to remain anonymous, I will respect your privacy as well. All I'm interested in is the facts and the truth."

Bennis stepped forward. "I met Sgt. Anthony many years ago in Ft. Benning, Georgia."

"Stop it, Jack! We need to think about this. It's freaking cold out here, and it's snowing. Maybe we can go to a diner and discuss this rationally over a cup of coffee."

Lucy Bauer nodded. But Father Bennis objected. "No. We need to stay here. Anthony's in there. He may need help."

"Anthony's in the funeral home?" Bauer asked. "What's he doing there? How did he get in? Why would he be in there?"

Cavanaugh shut his eyes and moaned. Then his cell phone rang again. Bauer, Bennis and Cavanaugh stiffened. The snow continued to flutter around them. Cavanaugh answered his phone.

It was Detective Goldberg.

* * * *

"You were right again, Suadela. We do, indeed, have company!"

Sgt. Anthony looked up to see a man dressed in a navy blue Scotch plaid hooded flannel bathrobe. His dark eyes seemed to glow beneath the hood. He wore white athletic socks. In his hand he held a 9MM "Black Widow" German

Luger.

"I recognize you," the voice beneath the hood said. "You were with the priest and that other man who was here yesterday. You look different, but I never forget a face. You wore a dirty Army jacket then."

Anthony calculated the distance between them. If he were closer, he could disarm him. At this distance, however, the scalpel was no contest against the Luger. He needed to get closer. He had severed the carotid artery of a few Viet Cong and one belligerent thief in a boarding house in Detroit. His knees cracked as he rose to his feet. He pointed to the floating heads on the shelf. "I see you like to save faces. What kind of a fucking nut are you anyhow?"

Grub moved a step closer. "Watch your language! You are in my house now."

Anthony took a step forward. He clutched the scalpel close to his thigh.

"Stay where you are! I saw your picture in the paper. The police are looking for you. They think you are the Staten Island Butcher." Grub started laughing. He waved his gun at Anthony. "If I shoot you, I will be a hero!"

"You're no fucking hero. A hero doesn't kidnap girls, torture them, and then slice them up like Swiss cheese. If you ask me, you're nothing but a warped, sadistic, worthless son of a bitch. You're lower than whale's shit in my book and a sorry-ass waste of life."

Otto Grub's hand shook. "You have no right to talk to me like that! When I kill you I will be a hero!"

Anthony laughed and moved a little closer. "If nobody knew I came in here, asshole, that might have worked. But that priest you mentioned and his obnoxious brother are both outside waiting for me. It's all over shit-head. You're not getting away with it this time."

Suadela whispered in Grub's ear. "Kill him. If you use the

Bio Cremation machine, you can bury his ashes with Jimmy Chen. No one will ever find his body."

"That's a great idea, Suadela." He started laughing again. His hand steadied. He looked at Anthony who had moved within eight feet of him. "What was it General MacArthur said in his farewell address, Suadela?"

Anthony tensed. One more step and then he would make his move slicing at Grub's carotid artery with the scalpel. "What the fuck are you talking about, numb-nuts?"

"Old soldiers never die. They just fade away."

The sharp, piercing sound of the Luger's report temporarily overshadowed Otto Grub's chilling laughter.

* * * *

Lucy Bauer and Tom Cavanaugh went into Father Bennis' car as the snow increased. Cavanaugh put his phone on speaker and spoke with Detective Goldberg. "Did you get the DNA results from the underwear?" Cavanaugh asked.

"There was a problem. Anthony's DNA is definitely on it, but some of the other DNA is partially corrupted. It looks like it might be DNA from the first victim found in Martlings' Pond, but we need to do more testing."

"We don't have time for more testing," Father Bennis shouted. "We need to go into the funeral home right now."

"Cavanaugh, is that your brother? What are you getting me into now? There's an APB out on him and Anthony."

Lucy Bauer sat quietly in the back seat taking notes.

"Listen, Morty, we may have jumped the gun a little, but you need to get a search warrant quick so we can go in there."

"And what possible reason am I supposed to give a judge that would warrant a search warrant of a funeral home? All the evidence points to Anthony as our serial killer."

"We think Otto Grub is the serial killer you're looking for, and he may still have Gretchen Leone in there somewhere."

"You have got to be kidding me! Otto Grub is a respected member of the community. You actually think a judge is going to give me a search warrant to go into his funeral home based on your *meshuggeneh* theory? No way, Cavanaugh!"

Lucy Bauer shouted from the backseat, "Malchus Anthony is in there!"

"Who's that?" Goldberg asked.

Cavanaugh glared at Bauer. "It's a CBS reporter. Her name is Lucy Bauer. You've probably seen her on TV."

"I don't believe it! What's she doing with you?"

"It's a long story, Morty, but she's right. Anthony snuck in there looking for the girl. He's been in there a while, and we haven't heard from him."

"Cavanaugh, this better not be another one of your pranks. If I come down there and find this is just a hoax to get me into the funeral home, I will gladly slap the cuffs on you and your brother!"

"It's no joke, Detective Goldberg," Father Bennis confirmed. "Malchus is in there."

"Please, put a rush on it, Morty. I'm beginning to get a bad feeling about Anthony and the girl."

"I'll do my best, but I'm going to have to go through channels on this one. It may take me a little time to get the okay. If he is in there, I don't want him slipping away on a technicality."

Cavanaugh looked out the car window. The snow had completely covered Anthony's footprints. "We're in the parking lot. Do what you have to do, but please hurry."

* * * *

Otto Grub worked fast. He stripped off Malchus Anthony's clothes. He laughed when he saw the Hawaiian sports shirt with pineapples and palm trees. "Look at this, Suadela. The only taste this man had was in his mouth."

"Shut up, Grub. Work faster. This is no time for show and tell. You have got to get him into that contraption of yours and then pulverize what's left of him."

Grub struggled to lift Anthony's limp body into his Bio Cremation machine. He ignored the lifeless body of Gretchen. Once Anthony's body was loaded, he filled the tank with water and an alkali solution of potassium hydroxide. He raised the temperature of the water to approximately 350 degrees, and then let the water, the alkali, the heat and the pressure in the tank do the rest. When he finished, he was sweating and his arms ached. He turned to Suadela and said, "I'll give it a few hours and then come back to grind the bones to dust in the cremulator. In the meantime, I still need to go back upstairs and clean the mess from the stink bombs. I wouldn't be surprised if that priest and his brother were somehow involved in that mess."

"Be careful, Grub. They suspect you."

"Once I dispose of these ashes, there will be no proof. I will even put his tasteless clothes beneath the cushioning of the casket. They can suspect me all they want, Suadela, but I am smarter than they are. I pay attention to details. They have no evidence." He patted the Bio Cremation machine. It was warm and he felt the pressure of the water swirling around Malchus Anthony's body. "There is no way they are going to stop me." As he wrapped his bathrobe tighter and headed upstairs to clean up Jimmy Chen's viewing room, he shouted to the walls, "There is no way anyone is going to stop me now!"

The Staten Island Butcher

He never saw Gretchen Leone's hand cautiously reach out for the scalpel on the floor.

* * * *

XII

The snow had stopped when Bennis, Cavanaugh, and Bauer saw a car's headlights coming into Grub's Funeral Home's parking lot. Cavanaugh looked at his watch. "I hope this is Goldberg. We need to get in there. This is taking too much time."

Father Bennis rolled down his window and leaned out. "We've got problems, Tom."

The car pulled alongside of them. A voice called out, "Well, what's the story?"

Cavanaugh opened his door and jumped out. "What the hell are you doing here?"

Greta Johnson ignored him and spoke to Bennis. "You told me you were going to call me. You didn't. What's going on?"

"We've had a few problems, Greta. You shouldn't be here."

"Well, I am. You promised you would get our granddaughter back. Where is she?"

In the backseat of Bennis' car, Lucy Bauer's eyes shifted from Johnson, to Cavanaugh, to Bennis as she continued to take notes.

"Go home, Mrs. Johnson," Cavanaugh said. "The police will be here soon. Everything is under control."

"I'm not going anywhere! Where's Gretchen? Is she in that building?" Her eyes surveyed the car. "Who's that in the back seat? And where is Anthony?"

"He went in there."

"That wasn't the plan!"

Lucy Bauer's hand stopped writing in midsentence. "What plan?"

"Who's she?" Greta asked peering into the back seat.

"This is Lucy Bauer. She's a reporter for CBS News," Bennis explained.

Cavanaugh shouted, "Put your pen down, Ms. Bauer, and you, Mrs. Johnson get out of your car and get in here and we'll explain everything."

When the four were settled in Bennis' car, Cavanaugh began. "This is all off the record, Ms. Bauer. We had reason to believe the owner of this funeral home is the serial killer the police are looking for."

"We saw him looking at the missing girl and when I visited the wake of Jimmy Chen I saw clothes that were burned in the gas fireplace."

"You'll never get a search warrant on that. That's not even circumstantial evidence. No judge in his right mind give you a search warrant on ludicrous assumptions like that."

"You're probably right about that. That's why your telling Detective Goldberg that Anthony is in there may get us in. You gave him probable cause to go into the building to arrest him."

"Even if this Detective Goldberg finds a sympathetic judge, they get a warrant for Anthony's arrest, and they go in there looking for Anthony, any evidence they find implicating Grub will be inadmissible."

"What are you? Some kind of lawyer or something?" Greta asked.

"I studied law in graduate school and I know the requirement for a warrant is probable cause. Did you actually see Anthony go into the funeral home?"

"Actually, no," Bennis said. "He knocked me out and shoved me in the trunk. Thomas was in the building when this happened."

"Then you didn't actually see him."

"No," Cavanaugh said, "but we followed his footprints to the fence in the back and saw he threw a wallet and a watch over the fence. Then we noticed he backtracked in his footprints to leave the impression that he jumped the fence."

Lucy Bauer and Greta Johnson looked out the car's windows. The heavier snow had covered all footprints. Greta shook her head and muttered, "We're screwed."

"Not necessarily," Cavanaugh said. "Under both the United States and New York constitutions, when a police officer applies for a warrant and has knowledge of facts given by a reasonably trustworthy source sufficient to create probably cause a warrant can be based on unsworn hearsay evidence."

"But nobody actually saw Anthony go into the building," Bennis said.

"Save your moral indignity for church, Jack. As far as Goldberg is concerned, I am a 'reasonably trustworthy source.' Once we get in there and find Anthony, trust me, we'll find proof that Otto Grub is the serial killer."

Father Bennis looked at his brother. "I don't like it. None of us actually saw Anthony go in there. What if he didn't go in there?"

"Look at it this way. Grub has murdered at least two

women we know about. Sophia Bellini and Gretchen are probably in there now. We don't know for sure what he has done to them. If we wait much longer, they might meet the same fate as the others. I'm more than willing to say I saw Anthony go in there if it will save their lives."

Greta Johnson checked her watch. "Why is it taking so long?"

"There should be no problem if a warrant for arrest has been issued for Anthony," Lucy Bauer stated. "In fact, there is actually no requirement that 'probable cause' to issue a search warrant be based on competent evidence. If I recall correctly, in New York State, at least, probable cause may be based on incompetent hearsay evidence."

"What if this Grub character refuses to let us in?"

"He may try, but that's why we need a warrant."

For the next three hours, they sat and waited in Bennis' car. The reporter tried to pry information out of the grandmother while Cavanaugh tried to deflect all questions. "Don't answer anything she asks. You have the right to remain silent. She's a reporter. I've seen how they work. Anything you say will be misquoted and then used against you."

"That's not true, Cavanaugh. I'm not like that."

"Ms. Bauer, I've seen your inquisitive nature. You can't help yourself. You remind me of a reporter I saw in a bar in Brooklyn a couple of years ago. She found herself next to a drunk who kept mumbling and studying something in his hand. She leaned closer while the drunk held the tiny object up to the light saying, 'It looks like plastic." Then he rolled it between his fingers. 'But it feels like rubber.' The reporter asked to take a look so the drunk handed it over and the reporter rolled it between her thumb and fingers, then sniffed it and licked it. 'You're right,' she said, 'it does look like plastic and feels like rubber, but it has no significant smell or taste. I don't know what it is. Where did you get it?' The drunk replied, 'Out of my nose.'"

The women said he was disgusting, but it didn't stop him and he continued. Father Bennis remained silent, staring at the building and praying for Anthony and Gretchen's safety.

* * * *

It wasn't until 4:30 a.m. that the first patrol cars arrived. Cavanaugh got out of the car to greet them. He recognized Patrolmen Mike Shanley and John Rhatigan whom he had worked with in Brooklyn. "What took you guys so long? We're been freezing our butts off waiting for you."

Shanley leaned out the passenger's side window. "Goldberg had a little trouble getting the warrant. The only judge he could find was a real hard ass who had just returned from a birthday party. He asked a lot of questions. Goldberg is finishing up the paperwork now. He should be here in a little while."

"How many cars have you got with you?"

"We have two out front. Me and Rhatigan are covering the back."

"You and Rhatigan are pretty close. Is there any truth in the rumor that you guys are somewhat romantically involved?"

Shanley glared at Cavanaugh. "How can you joke at a time like this? We're here to arrest a serial killer and all you do is joke?"

"I guess you could say I'm incorrigible, but you probably wouldn't know what that meant. I'm sorry. I guess it's a nervous habit I have when things get tense. By the way, did you hear about the Irish newlyweds who sat up all night on their honeymoon waiting for their sexual relations to arrive?"

Rhatigan stepped on the accelerator and sped around

the end of the building toward the delivery entrance as Shanley waved one of his fingers at Cavanaugh.

* * * *

At 5:15 a.m. Goldberg arrived with three more squad cars. "Has he come out yet?" he asked Cavanaugh.

"No."

Goldberg scanned the building. "You can't see entrances or exits from where you are. What makes you so sure he didn't come out?"

"I'm telling you he's in there. Trust me. I know he's in there."

"You don't know what I had to do to get this warrant. My *tochis* is on the line here. If this is another of your *farchadat* theories, I'm going to make life miserable for you."

"When do you plan to go in?"

Goldberg checked his watch. "Sunrise is around 7:00 a.m. I figure we'll wait until then. I don't like going in in the dark. Too many bad things can happen."

"A lot of bad things can happen between now and 7:00," Father Bennis said. "He's got Anthony and two women in there. We need to act quickly."

"Allegedly, Father. "

"Are you going to risk the lives of three people waiting for the sun to come out?" a female voice from the backseat of the car asked.

Goldberg peered in. "Who's she?"

"She's Lucy Bauer, a CBS reporter."

Greta Johnson got out on the other side of the car and waved her finger at Goldberg. "My granddaughter may be in there, Detective. You promised you would help find her. What kind of policeman are you who is afraid of the dark? If anything happens to my granddaughter...."

George R. Hopkins

Goldberg raised his hand in mock surrender. He radioed the units that he was preparing to go in with the warrant for Anthony's arrest. He advised all to be on the alert. "Anthony could be dangerous. Use caution. If possible we would like to take him alive. Use deadly force only if necessary."

* * * *

Suadela spoke softly to Grub. "The police are here. They have the building surrounded. Finish what you started."

"I can't let them in here. They'll find Gretchen."

"They have no plausible reason to suspect you. They are looking for the old soldier. You have nothing to worry about."

"I should have done away with Gretchen, too."

"There was no time to get rid of her body. She is in your secret playroom. We'll get rid of her tonight. Then you can go get that college professor. I think she's more your type."

Grub gathered the ashes of Sophia Bellini and Malchus Anthony and headed up to Jimmy Chen's viewing room. He opened the casket and moved Jimmy to the side. He carefully distributed the fine dust-like powder under the casket lining and in Jimmy's pockets.

"I didn't realize there would be so much ashes." He rolled the body over and spread the last of the ashes under the corpse. Then he rolled the body back, repositioned it and admired his work.

"Snap out of it, asshole. The police will be knocking on your door any minute now."

"I thought you said I had nothing to worry about."

"Look at your hands, stupid. You have human remains all over them. Wash your hands. A little water will clear you of all evidence."

Grub smiled. He had cleared the room of stink bombs from the previous night. He had hidden the remains of

Sophia Bellini and Malchus Anthony in Jimmy Chen's casket. He used a hand vacuum to eliminate any white dust on Jimmy's clothes and around the area. Before closing the lid, he leaned over and placed Jimmy's left hand over his right. Otto Grub prided himself on his attention to detail.

He threw his clothes in the washing machine and jumped into the shower. Suadela was there with him. As the water cascaded over him, he started to laugh. "You are right, Suadela. There is nothing I have to worry about. I am smarter than all of them. We have devised the perfect way to dispose of our victims. Ashes to ashes and dust to dust. I am invincible!"

*　*　*　*

XIII

The police pounded on the front door of Grub's Funeral Home for five minutes. They were about to break the door down when Otto Grub appeared. He was dressed in a white terrycloth bathrobe. His hair was wet and he was barefooted. "What's with all the noise? You would think you were trying to wake up the dead."

Goldberg presented Grub with a warrant to search the funeral home looking for a murder suspect named Malchus Anthony. "I can assure you, Detective, this Malchus Anthony is not in here. I have an elaborate security system. Surely, I would have been notified of his presence."

"We have eye witness accounts that he did enter your building."

Grub stood steadfast holding the door with one hand and the warrant in the other. "Surely, you must know that so called 'confident witnesses' are wrong at least 30% of the time."

"My name is not Shirley, Mr. Grub. It's Detective Morton

Goldberg and our warrant is to look for and apprehend Malchus Anthony."

"This is an established Funeral Home, Detective Goldberg. I resent having police invade my home on an alleged statement that fugitive is hiding on my premises."

"If you are refusing to allow us entry, I will make a note of that in my report. And then we will begin our search for Anthony with or without your permission. I would have thought you would be more cooperative in working with the police to apprehend a dangerous killer."

Grub stood still for a moment, checked the warrant again, and then slowly opened the door. "Please be respectful. We have a deceased in the viewing room. His burial is scheduled for later this morning."

Goldberg gave the signal and a squad of twelve police officers invaded Grub's Funeral Home. "Be careful," Goldberg warned. "Search everywhere he might be hiding. He could be dangerous." As the police began their search, Cavanaugh and Bennis appeared at the door with Greta Johnson and Lucy Bauer behind them.

* * * *

The police scoured the Grub Funeral Home for the next three hours. Paul Scamardella, Mike Marotta, Steve Impellizzieri, and Dennis Coppolino arrived early to assist in Jimmy Chen's funeral and burial. They joined Cavanaugh, Bennis, Johnson, and Bauer at the main entrance. "What's going on?" Marotta asked.

"They are looking for Malchus Anthony. He's a murder suspect. They think he snuck in when delivering flowers," the reporter volunteered.

Scamardella asked, "Is he the guy that mugged me? I want to get my hands on him."

"Your watch and wallet are in the bushes out back," Cavanaugh said. "We think he doubled back and went in looking for Gretchen Leone."

"You think?"

"Apparently, no one actually saw him go in," Bauer said, "but Mr. Cavanaugh insists he did."

Detective Goldberg appeared at the front door. "We have searched this place high and low. There is absolutely no sign of Anthony. Cavanaugh, I told you I went out on a limb for you, but now you're going to pay for wasting police time and energy, not to mention upsetting a respected member of the community."

"Did you check the fireplace? Did you see the burnt clothes in it?" Cavanaugh asked.

"The warrant was for Anthony's arrest, not an inspection of Grub's fireplace."

"I know he's in there, Morty. You've got to believe me. Let me look."

Mourners for Jimmy Chen's funeral began to arrive. "I should lock you up right now, but I'll let you go in and pay your respects. Then we're going to the station. I will be right behind you so don't try any of your tricks."

*   *   *   *

Otto Grub watched the mourners file in to pay their final respects to Jimmy Chen. When he saw Cavanaugh, Father Bennis, and Detective Goldberg proceed into the viewing room, he felt his heart skip a beat. He started to sweat. He looked around. Where was Suadela? He needed her.

He stood like a statue and watched Cavanaugh point to the fireplace where he had burned Sophia and Gretchen's clothes. His hands were shaking. Where had Suadela gone?

He saw Kim Daggett and her husband arrive and talk

with Cavanaugh, the detective, and the priest. He felt perspiration on his forehead. What were they talking about? Why had Suadela abandoned him? Where was she? He needed her.

Then the group approached the closed casket. He heard Cavanaugh ask if they had looked inside the casket. Detective Goldberg motioned to one of the police officers who shook his head no. Grub wanted to run. He eased himself over to the door leading to the basement. He tried to blend into the wallpaper.

There was a brief conversation with Kim Daggett and then a police sergeant leaned over and opened Jimmy Chen's casket. Grub held his breath. He had taken care to vacuum any of Sophia and Anthony's ashes away. They were looking for Anthony. He was nothing more than a fine dust now. They were never going to find him. Suadela was right. He had nothing to worry about. But he could hear his heart pumping. Where was Suadela? Time seemed to crawl backward.

He watched the group look at Jimmy Chen's corpse. They seemed satisfied. The police sergeant made a move to close the casket. But Cavanaugh suddenly shouted, "Stop! The body has been moved."

"What are you talking about?" Detective Goldberg said.

"Look at his hands. When I was here before his hands were in a different position."

Kim Daggett leaned over. "Yes. He's right. His hands are reversed. Jimmy's right hand was covering his left and the pinkie finger he broke playing basketball. Now the broken finger is on top."

Grub planned to explain the body had been moved in the cleanup process from the previous night, but before he could Cavanaugh reached in and moved the body. Fine white dust clung to Jimmy's back and spilled out from his pocket. How was he going to explain this? He looked around for Suadela, but she was gone.

He opened the door to run. Then he saw it. He screamed. A ghost-like figure shrouded in white reached out for him. It slashed at his neck. He felt the cold steel severing his carotid artery. Blood exploded forward splattering the white specter before him. "Suadela?" he cried. Grabbing his neck in a futile attempt to stop the bleeding, he fell to his knees. Darkness closed in on him. "Why, Suadela? Why?"

The figure in white bent over him. He saw the bloody scalpel. Then he looked into her eyes. It wasn't Suadela. He felt an eerie coldness seeping over him as the voice beneath the white taffeta lining whispered, "May the devil cut off the rest of your head when you go to hell, you sadistic son of a bitch!" He never heard the people running toward him. He didn't have time to figure out how it happened, but he knew before he died Gretchen Leone had killed him.

* * * *

The police rushed to the stairwell. They found Otto Grub bleeding out and Gretchen standing over him with a bloody scalpel. She dropped the scalpel when she saw the police. She had Grub's blood all over the white lining covering her. One of her eyes was severely bruised and the other swollen shut. Her nose looked like it had been broken and one of her front teeth was missing. Her grandmother pushed through the crowd and hugged her. Goldberg called in for an ambulance. Cavanaugh led Gretchen to a chair and asked what happened. Father Bennis hung back by Jimmy Chen's casket and watched.

Gretchen rambled on between bouts of tears about how she was abducted on the way home from work, how he beat her, how he used a machine in a secret room downstairs to dissolve Sophia's body and that of the older man who came to rescue her. When she started to tell them about the floating heads he kept as trophies or souvenirs, she became hysterical. When the EMTs arrived, two police officers helped escort Gretchen to the ambulance. On the way out, Gretchen was sobbing, "I saw him shoot the man! I saw him shoot the man!"

Greta insisted on going with her, but Goldberg refused to allow her to go with them. Gretchen had killed Otto Grub and was now in police custody. He assured her she would be able to talk to her as soon as her medical issues were dealt with. She turned and looked around her. The room was in chaos. People were milling around and talking. She saw Jack Bennis standing by the casket talking to his brother. She went over to him and said, "Thank you."

Initially, she didn't think he heard her. He was talking to Cavanaugh. "When you first saw Sgt. Anthony, Thomas, you saw an alcoholic, a dishonorable soldier, and a failure." He reached in and picked up some of the fine white dust on the cushioning in the casket. "He was more than that, much more than that. The problem is I think most of us suffer from some form of pareidolia."

"What is 'pareidolia'? I never heard of it before," Greta said.

Cavanaugh answered, "My brother likes to use big words, Mrs. Johnson. Pareidolia is a psychological term to describe how the mind tends to see a familiar pattern in some things where none actually exists. Our minds are programed to detect meaning in patterns, and we infer or assume relationships from coincidences. The end result is we think we understand what is causing the patterns, but we really have no idea."

"You mean like they say when you assume, you make an 'ass' out of 'you' and 'me'?"

"Something like that, Greta," Bennis said. "We have all heard of it: the potato chip that looked like Elvis; the hot cross bun that resembled Mother Teresa; the oil stain on the highway that tied up traffic because people thought it was an apparition of the Virgin Mary; the tomato that looked like a portrait of Jesus." He let Anthony's ashes flow through his hands. "It's one thing to think we see an image where none really exists, but quite another thing when we make assumptions about people."

"But assumptions aren't always false. I knew you would help find Gretchen when you learned she was your granddaughter."

"That's true, but she really isn't my granddaughter, is she?"

"What do you mean?"

"Anthony didn't go into this funeral home for no reason. He risked his life when he didn't have to. I wondered why he would do that. Then I remembered his last words to me. 'Don't trust her.'"

I don't understand, Jack."

"I think you do, Greta. You wanted to find your granddaughter. I can't blame you for that. You were willing to do whatever you could to get her home safely. To do that, you used what you knew about me to get me to help."

Greta Johnson turned away. "This is ridiculous. I don't have to listen to this. We have our granddaughter back. That's all that matters now."

Jack Bennis reached out and grasped her shoulders. "You hated Malchus not because of what he did to your friend, but for what he did to you. Malchus gave his life to save Gretchen. You owe me the truth, Greta. And you owe Gretchen the truth, too. I don't want to put her through a DNA test to discover her grandmother is a liar. What really happened between you and Malchus?"

Greta's shoulders started to tremble. She started sniffling. He turned her around and looked at her. Her eyes were watery and dark mascara-laced tears began to roll down her cheeks. "I didn't mean to hurt anyone. He wasn't supposed to go in there. That wasn't part of the plan."

"But he did."

She looked at the fine white dust in Bennis' hands. "When I saw him, I panicked. I didn't want him to tell you the truth. I was afraid you would stop looking for Gretchen."

Bennis led Greta to a chair and they both sat down. "Tell me what really happened. Did he rape you?"

"No." She held her hands to her eyes. "Nothing happened between you and me. After talking all night, you fell asleep. I thought we would have sex, but you were out cold. I was looking forward to it. When I left the motel room, I saw Anthony. He gave me some money. I think it was actually your money. And then he told me to go home. I ... I didn't want to go home. I told him it was still early and asked him if there was anything else we could do. He looked at me like he didn't know what to say. Then ... then I guess I came on to him."

Bennis rubbed his forehead.

"I told you a girl doesn't forget her first. Malchus Anthony was my first."

"Was he Gretchen's grandfather?"

Greta looked up at the priest and nodded.

Bennis reached over and held her hands. "He remembered you, too. That's why he went along with your story about raping a friend on a pile of manure. He was playing the macho role as much for you as for me. I saw the way he was looking at the pictures in your house of you and your daughter. Malchus had a tough life, and I am sure a lot of regrets."

"Now you are assuming, Jack."

"You're right, but he did tell me about some of his experiences which haunted him at night. Drinking was a way to block out those memories. He spoke about being a 'bad tree.' That was an assumption he made about himself. From the stories he told me, however, I think his assumption about himself was wrong. I don't think he was what he and a lot of other people thought he was. He was definitely rough around the edges, but inside, I think, he tried to do the right thing. Life is definitely not fair, and surviving on the streets can be cruel. Basically, he had a good heart, but no heart is strong enough to hold a bullet."

* * * *

XIV

By early December, Otto Grub was old news. Christmas decorations had been up since before Thanksgiving, but all the early snow had melted as Lonnie Quinn, John Elliot, Janice Huff, and Jim Cantore continued to talk about the lingering effects of *El Niño* and global warming. Little Stephen Cavanaugh was asleep and Tom and Fran Cavanaugh were watching a re-run of *Midsummer Murders* when the doorbell rang. It was Fr. Jack Bennis. In his hands he balanced a white clam pie from Denino's, a six pack of Becks beer and a bottle of Reasons white wine.

"What's all this?" Fran asked.

"I just wanted to thank you guys for helping to find Gretchen and to check in on how my godson Stephen is doing?"

"He's doing fine. The doctors say he has shown no adverse effects from Kawasaki disease. How are you doing?"

Bennis plopped down on the sofa. Cavanaugh turned off the T.V. Fran brought out some glasses and plates.

"I hope I'm not bothering you both. I was curious if you found out anything new about Otto Grub."

Cavanaugh took his key chain out and popped open two bottles of Becks. "Goldberg told me they were able to identify the first two victims from dental records in the heads they found in Grub's secret room. They were both runaways. One was a sixteen year old girl from Indiana and the other one was an eighteen year old from Tennessee. Gretchen told how Sgt. Anthony freed her and how she played dead. It probably saved her life. She saw Grub shoot Anthony point-blank in the chest and then put him in some machine that dissolved his flesh. Then he ground his bones into a fine dust which he placed in Jimmy Chen's casket. "

"She's a brave girl," Fran said. "I don't know what I would do in her place."

"The doctors say she suffered a few broken bones and a lot of trauma. Physically, she should do all right. Emotionally, who knows?'

Bennis took a long swig from his beer bottle. "If she's anything like her grandmother, she should do all right."

Fran opened the bottle of wine and poured a glass for herself. "Tom, tell Jack about that other woman?"

"What other woman?"

"Well, that's just it. We don't know. Gretchen told the police she heard Grub talking to a woman he called Suadela, but there was no sign of her in the funeral home."

Fran said, "I think she escaped in the confusion."

"Goldberg didn't think that was possible. The police were surrounding the place and they questioned everyone leaving. He said they found no evidence of another woman's presence in the entire building."

"Maybe Gretchen imagined it. Under stress we sometimes hear and see things that aren't there."

"Maybe, but some witnesses swear they heard Grub talking to this Suadela in the stairwell. Goldberg thinks it was part of a psychotic disorder Grub suffered from. He thinks he may have had some form of schizophrenia that affected his behavior and resulted in hallucinations and delusions. He thinks he was seeing and hearing things like David Berkowitz, the Son of Sam, claimed. Apparently, Grub, like Berkowitz, was a loner who was known to have a mean streak of bullying and teasing others growing up. The skull they found in Grub's secret room turned out to be his mother's."

Bennis started to tear the label off his beer bottle. "What do you think, Thomas?"

"I had a chance to check his office and saw he had some books on Greek tragedy. One of the books was *Twelve Months in Peitho's Den.* In Greek mythology, Peitho was the goddess of persuasion and seduction. Her Roman name was Suadela. I think Grub read too many of these myths and in his sick mind he thought Suadela may have been talking to him, persuading him to do the things he did."

Bennis rubbed the scar on his forehead and then reached for another bottle of beer.

"There you go again, Jack, with that 'tell' of yours. What does my big brother think?"

Bennis folded his pizza slice and took a large bite. "I love Denino's pizza."

"We almost forgot, Jack. You had a couple of letters addressed to you from Colombia. With all that's been going on, we forgot to give them to you." She got up and handed him two letters from the dining room table. One was typed and the other handwritten. He looked at the letters, but said nothing.

"Come on, Jack, what do you think about Suadela?" Fran asked.

He closed his eyes and chewed slowly before he answered. "I'm not sure you want to hear my theory. It's a bit different." He put the letters in his pocket and began. "Thomas, do you remember that when we went into The Waterview Grub had two glasses of white wine in front of him?"

"Yeah, I thought he was some kind of alcoholic."

"Well, I asked Gretchen about it when I visited her in the hospital. She said he was waiting for someone, but when we showed up, he only ordered one meal. I think Suadela saw me."

"That's crazy. There was nobody there."

"What if there was, but we didn't see her? What if she was afraid I might recognize her for what she was?"

"Now you have completely lost me!"

"Gretchen remembered some of the things Grub said to her. He said something about seeing others suffer does one good and that he wanted her to abandon her moral center. Why would he say that?"

"Maybe because he was a sick bastard!"

Fran asked, "What do you think, Jack?"

"The Son of Sam claimed he received messages to kill from a demon-possessed dog. What if Suadela was an evil spirit that possessed him?"

"Now you've really lost me! You actually think Grub was possessed by the Devil? I thought they did away with the Devil along with Limbo a long time ago."

Bennis took a deep breath. "There's a lot of evil in the world. No one can deny that. All you have to do is look around you. An eighty-year-old man is mugged for fun by a group of teenagers; an eight-year-old girl is killed in a random drive-by shooting; a ninety-two-year-old woman is

222

beaten and raped in her stairwell. The Bible tells us to be sober-minded and watchful for the Devil is our adversary and prowls around like a roaring lion seeking someone to devour. He can take many forms. It tells us that Satan can disguise himself as an angel of light. Sometimes he can come in the guise of power, wealth, or freedom. But the Devil is there. You were a cop, Thomas. You saw it every day. Perhaps I see and hear too much of it in my daily work. But yes, I do believe there is palpable evil in the world. You can call it what you will, but I call it the Devil."

There was silence in the room for a few minutes. They each sipped their drinks and ate their pizza. Then Fran spoke. "So let me get this straight. I think Suadela escaped. Goldberg thinks Suadela was part of Grub's psychotic disorder. Tom thinks Suadela is some unconscious hallucination of the Roman goddess of persuasion and seduction. And Jack thinks Suadela is an evil spirit that possessed Grub."

"That about sums it up. I guess we will never really know. At least not in this world."

Fran topped off her glass of wine. "It scares me to think there are Suadelas wandering around out there – whatever they are. What kind of a crazy world is our Stephen growing up in?"

Fr. Bennis lifted his bottle of beer and clicked it with his brother's and Fran's glass. "Here's to the hope that people all over the world will one day soon learn to love their neighbors as themselves and respect their right to follow their own beliefs in peace and harmony. And may God bless us all."

Just as they all said, "Amen," Stephen woke up and started to cry.

* * * *

George R. Hopkins

The Staten Island Butcher

ABOUT THE AUTHOR

George Hopkins is a native New York who has lived and worked in all five boroughs of New York City. This novel takes place in Staten Island where he now lives. Sometimes called the "Forgotten Borough," Staten Island is the least populated of the five boroughs of New York City, but it is the third largest with thousands of acres of park lands. Hopkins has won awards for his teaching, his television productions, and his novels and poetry. He was a sergeant in the United States Marine Corps Reserves.

The Staten Island Butcher is the seventh suspense/thriller/mystery in his priest and homicide detective brothers' series. Other novels in this series include: *Blood Brothers, Collateral Consequences, Letters from the Dead, Random Acts of Malice, Unholy Retribution,* and *Chasing the Devil's Breath.* All these books are available at Amazon.com and Barnes & Noble.com and can be ordered from bookstores.

He welcomes the opportunity to answer questions and to speak at book clubs, book stores, and other groups about his novels and about the writing process. You may contact him at his email address: Hopkins109@aol.com . His website is www.george-hopkins.com, and his author's page on Amazon is amazon.com/author/georgehopkins.

If you find the time, please write a brief review at Amazon.com or Barnes and Noble.com about *The Staten Island Butcher.*

Thank you.

Made in the USA
Middletown, DE
10 September 2018